DARK MERCY

/ / / /

J.R. RAIN
&
MATTHEW S. COX

MADDY WIMSEY SERIES

The Devil's Eye
The Drifting Gloom
Dark Mercy

Published by
Crop Circle Books
212 Third Crater, Moon

Printed in the United States of America.

ISBN-9781071133170

Chapter One
Rough

Lucky to have a relatively light week, I wind up catching a suicide jumper.

Unfortunately, I didn't actually catch the guy. Just his case. Catching the actual guy in this situation would've been bad for both of us. Well, mostly bad for me. He'd have been dead either way.

Despite the somberness of the scene, my mood remains high. Caius finally proposed to me not too long ago and I'm still flying high from that. However, out of respect for the dead, I am totally capable of not smiling here. Mostly. At least my hair has my back so to speak. She keeps blowing into my face whenever I randomly think about Caius or the upcoming wedding—which we still haven't set a date for—or the squeal my friend Isabelle made when she saw me accept. A good night, all around.

Rick and I are presently standing on the sidewalk in the shadow of a high-rise office building in downtown Olympia, gazing up at the very roof where we were told he had jumped from. Sunlight shimmers on a strip of silver at the edge, making me squint. It's a pity that the guy picked a nice day to do this. Clear skies and sun aren't the norm here.

The remains of one Mr. Archibald Montgomery, age thirty-four, rest beneath a fluttering blue tarp beside Rick and me. A starburst of red covers the sidewalk well in excess of what the plastic can hide. Thirty feet away on the opposite side of the street, the rear end of a green Volvo sticks out from the window of a cupcake bakery. Most people wouldn't draw any connection between a suicide jumper and a woman putting her car through the wall of a shop. But I also don't think like most people. She probably saw him falling, got distracted, and lost control.

"What do you make of this?" asks a patrol officer to Rick's left.

My partner peels his gaze off the roof, glances at the tarp, and shrugs. "Pretty sure he's dead. That's about all I'm gonna get just from looking at the scene before speaking to anyone."

I glance at the cop. "You have statements or information from witnesses?"

The officer nods. "Yeah. A handful, mostly from street level. No one noticed the guy until he hit the ground. Driver of the Volvo didn't have much to add. Only that a piece of, uhh, 'debris' hit her windshield. She started vomiting, lost control, strayed over the line into the oncoming lane. A bus objected to her trespass and punted the Volvo into the cupcake place like Ronaldo tryin' to score from midfield."

"Ouch." I cringe. "So no one you talked to knew the deceased? No idea why he jumped?"

Rick whistles. "If my name was Archibald, I'd throw myself off a building, too."

"Nah." The cop ignores my partner's comment, continuing to look at me. "He's got an ID badge for an architectural drawing firm that has office space here, but aside from a couple people saying he'd been acting a little out of it this morning, no one had any idea what made him do it. Have fun with this one, detectives."

"Yeah…" I look around the scene again. "Who told you he went off the roof if no one saw him until he hit the sidewalk?"

The cop gestures at the building's entrance. "Security people. They got him on video going out to the roof, but the dude didn't hesitate at all. Just went straight to the edge, climbed the little wall, and leapt. The security people hadn't even made it halfway up the building before he was in free fall."

"Whatever went wrong for this guy, he wasn't trying to make a cry for help. He took an express elevator to hell. Going down." Rick glances sideways at me. "Not an *Aliens* fan? Never mind."

"Oh, brother," I mutter. "Okay, thank you,

Officer Coleman."

He nods.

Leaving him there to guard the body with the other cops, we head inside to the desk in the lobby. Though it has four seats and four computers, only one guy in a black 'security' polo shirt is there. Soft murmuring comes from a hallway behind the counter that I assume to be for the security staff, as it's small and plain compared to the elevator area to the left, which is full of modernist corporate prettiness, like long marble tables and vases with fresh cut flowers.

We show our badges and introduce ourselves to the one guy there, Mark Kohl. He's clearly rattled from having a front-row seat to a man committing suicide. I don't expect we'll have to make them hold off on cleaning the blood spatter from the building's front windows too much longer if that video checks out.

"We'd like to see the video from the roof if possible," I say.

"Oh, sure, this way." Mark stands.

He leads us over to the plain hallway and to a room lined with small monitors and recording equipment, also two other people: a visibly upset fiftyish black woman and a late-twenties Latina who's trying to console her. Evidently, the older woman also witnessed Archibald's landing. Both are wearing security polos. Mark introduces us.

Rick nods, flashing his badge. "Did any of you know Mr. Montgomery?" The older black lady shakes her head first. "No. Only that the man worked here, upstairs. Just not the kinda thing I ever expected to see happen right in front of me."

Rick makes sympathetic sounds and glances at the others. "How about you two?"

They reply no.

"Did any of you observe anything unusual today or recently regarding him?" I ask.

All three of the security staff shake their heads.

"Guy didn't really stand out," says the Hispanic woman.

"Gonna show them the video." Mark sits in one of the black-cushioned office chairs and clicks his way past login prompts and menu options.

The older woman turns her back. "I can't watch that again."

Mark points at the screen, broken into eight sub-panels each with a different security feed. Two show the roof from different angles, the rest, hallways, cubicles, and a break area.

"Impressive. You watch every square foot of this place, huh?" asks Rick.

"Not in real time." Mark clicks a box and enters a time code. "It's recorded though. Usually, the video is used for exactly this... looking at stuff after the fact. We've got a few hot feeds up front, critical locations that we monitor real time. But ninety-five percent of it is just recorded in case we need it later. External doors, the back alley and the roof access are monitored in real time. That's why we tried hoofing it to the roof to stop the guy, but the elevator would've needed a rocket engine to get us up there fast enough."

A figure I recognize (mostly from the driver's license photo and coat as the body was in bad shape) walks down the hallway in one of the camera views. He doesn't appear to be in an elevated emotional state, calmly strolling to a doorway marked 'no entrance.' A faint flicker of light glints behind him seconds before he pushes the door open and enters a stairwell.

Whoa. What was that?

Frowning, I watch as he emerges from a door captured by an external camera, walks straight off the bend in the path to a helipad, and climbs a four-foot high wall at the edge. He's over and gone in seconds.

"Wow. That guy really wanted to jump. No hesitation whatsoever," mutters Rick.

"Can you back up to 9:42:18?" I ask.

Mark clicks on an arrow, rewinding to a second before I noticed the odd flash.

"Frame by frame it?"

Nodding, Mark advances the video one frame at a time. A fist-sized spot of light floats into the image from the left and slips behind Archibald, not coming out the other side of his head. Either it disappeared behind him or went *into* him.

"Oh, hey," says Mark. "That looks like one of those 'light anomalies' from some ghost hunting show."

"Or a lens flare." Maria, the younger of the two

women, points at it. "Just the camera catching the overhead lights."

Mark shakes his head. "This isn't a Michael Bay or J.J. Abrams movie. That's not a lens flare. Sorry, I take film classes at school."

Rick chuckles, but gives me side eye.

"Can we go up and look at the spot?" I ask. "And if you can send us a copy of this video, it would be a big help."

"Sure. You want me to email a file or do you have a flash drive?"

"Email works." I give him my departmental email for public contact.

Once he's sent the file, he leads us back to the elevators and we go upstairs. Despite the hallway to the roof stairs being well lit an hour before noon, it's radiating a vibe like a haunted house. Nothing visible sets off my warning bells—and my hair doesn't decide to grab onto anything—so I don't quite go on high alert. This feels more like something *was* here, the kind of something that I can't put in any police report and expect to keep my job. When we reach the outside door leading to the roof, a weird chill slithers down my back like a lump of slime.

I spin, but there's no one behind me poking me with a piece of raw fish. It's an odd sensation that's quite new to me. I'm not sure if I sensed something in the air like a residual imprint or if an entity actively touched me.

A squeak announces the door opening; strong

sunlight floods the stairwell. Rick leads the way forward onto the roof. The security guy gives us a brief tour of the area, including a few seconds' peek over the side. It's difficult to see the remains from this high up, but it's pretty obvious we're directly above the front entrance where he landed.

"This looks like a pretty clear-cut case of suicide," says Rick.

While I have my doubts, I like being employed. "Let's go talk to the co-workers."

Rick nods.

We head to the thirty-fourth floor and the office of Hartman & Dunn, the design firm where Archibald used to work. It takes up roughly a quarter of the floor. Mark stays in the elevator and continues on to the lobby below while we make our way down the hall to the firm.

Rick pulls open the metallic door for me. "You know, Wims, you're starting to see ghosts everywhere."

"Paranormal stuff *is* everywhere, Rick. Most people simply ignore it as a reflex."

"Or it was just a light glitch."

"Maybe."

"I'm sensing a but here..."

I grin. "But if that *was* a spirit, it might have simply sensed the man was about to die and came to check it out."

"I love how you talk about this stuff like it's so normal."

I sigh out my nose. As superstitious as cops are,

you'd think a girl could air her suspicion that a spirit might have been involved in causing a death without ending up in a mandatory psych evaluation. The sense that something more than simple severe depression killed this guy gnaws at me, but there's not much to go on. Most of the time when a person is killed by powers beyond our understanding, the person has brought it on themselves. I can't help but think of Elise, the youngest member of my coven, and her run-in with a dangerous negative entity. Part of me thinks the only reason she survived is that she hadn't intended to summon that thing. It forced its way past the gate she opened while trying to contact her dead mother.

Rick reaches the desk first, holding up his badge. "Detective Rick Santiago, and this is Detective Madeline Wimsey. We're here regarding Archibald Montgomery."

"Oh, right," says the fellow redhead behind the desk. She's late thirties with a pinkish complexion. Her hair's nowhere near as epic as mine though, straight and thin. She's visibly upset over the news. Indeed, the entire office looks shaken.

"We'd like to speak with his manager and anyone you feel may have known him." I put my badge away and offer a comforting smile. "We can start with you, if you knew him."

"Not really. He kept to himself. Never saw him at the Christmas parties." The woman exhales. "Hold on, I think he worked under Martin. Let me check the org chart."

We wait a moment.

"Yep. One sec. I'll be right back." The woman gets up and hurries off down a hall.

"Gonna be rough," mutters Rick.

"Why's that? She barely knew him."

"No, I mean it's the first of August. Any month that starts off with a suicide is going to be rough."

Maybe I am jumping at shadows, as Rick suggested. No matter what, this is going down as a suicide. The video is compelling and clear. The question, for me, is what led him to make such a dramatic decision. Had something influenced him to jump? And had that something been supernatural in nature? Yes, I'm looking at you weird light anomaly. Hell, even if I can find enough evidence to convince myself that someone may have sent a spiritual assassin after him, the death is *still* going down as an official suicide.

Did I mention I like my job?

Yeah. I'd rather keep it.

Chapter Two
Concerned Citizen

Well, that's one way to blow an afternoon.

Rick and I spent four hours at the design firm talking to anyone and everyone who had ever known Archibald existed. People who sat near him described him as quiet but friendly. He didn't go out of his way to meet people or initiate conversation, but would be pleasant with anyone who needed to talk to him. His manager described him as a 'slightly above average' employee. Competent and reasonably motivated, but no all-star. However, his utter lack of causing drama, complaining, or drawing attention to himself—plus never taking sick days—endeared him to management.

We dug deeper throughout the day. He had no surviving family, being an only child whose parents and grandparents had all died years ago. Based on the ages of death for the parents, he came along late. Nothing looks screwy in his finances, no pets, and no last will. No one stood to gain anything from his death as far as I can tell, and his apartment didn't contain anything outlandish—just a personal art studio with lots of drawings of flowers, landscapes, and still-lifes.

Worst of all, no note.

So, yeah. Although suicide is the official cause of death of poor Mr. Archibald Montgomery, I still don't know *why* he offed himself. Which, admittedly, is frustrating as hell.

I'm almost done filling out the reports for that when my desk phone chimes. It's an internal ringtone, so that means it's either Captain Janet Greer or the desk sergeant. Suppose it could be anyone in the building, really, but I can't think of anyone other than those two people who would be calling me direct.

I pick up the receiver. "Homicide, Wimsey."

"Detective," says Sergeant Dale Cridlin, the poor bastard at the front desk. "Got someone here asking to speak to a homicide detective about a possible murder. You're the only one picking up."

"One sec." I lean back in my chair to check out my colleagues' desks. Sure enough, Rick and I *are* the only ones here. Granted, I don't have anything else to do than finishing up a report. At least, anything else pressing. The past two weeks have been scarily quiet from a murder standpoint. I really hope the city isn't building up for a shitstorm. "Give me like five minutes?"

"No problem, detective."

I hang up and go back to typing up the report, only faster.

"What's that about?" asks Rick.

"Not sure yet. Someone wants to report a possible murder."

He chuckles. "Possible? Probably the milk jugs in a garbage bag prank again."

"If only." I smile at the memory. Some idiots had been stuffing empty milk bottles in garbage bags and tying them closed to approximate the shape of a human body. They'd leave the dummies around town to freak people out.

Three minutes later, I close the report file with some reluctance. I'm still not totally convinced everything about that man's death *was* a suicide, but it's difficult to argue with the video. No one held a gun to his head or physically threw him over the edge. The man quite clearly jumped of his own— and rather eager—accord. But, the feeling, specifically that slimy mass creeping down my back, tells me a different story. Nothing I can do about it now. Everyone already thinks I'm a little eccentric. If I start rambling on about paranormal entities influencing people to jump off buildings, it wouldn't go well for my career. I'd be lucky to end up assigned to one of those little golf cart things, handing out parking tickets.

I make my way through the somewhat labyrinthine hallways of the precinct to the front room. The usual arrangement of people sit around the benches: some are waiting in hopes of seeing an arrested relative, others stand in line awaiting their turn to complain about something ridiculous like chicken nuggets being cold. There are a handful of lawyers, some people with actual complaints, and the occasional homeless person who just wants to sit somewhere out of the rain for a little while.

Exactly... rain. Clear skies just a few hours earlier—now it's raining buckets. Welcome to the Northwest.

"What'cha got?" I ask, walking up behind the desk.

Sergeant Cridlin's a big guy. Ex-Army, from Texas as far as I know, about six-four and probably over three hundred pounds. Figure they put him on the front desk because almost no one would want to mess with him.

"Over there, the strawberry blonde. Kaitlyn Underwood." He indicates a woman with a nod. "Says she has information about a killer."

"Thanks." I pat him on the shoulder and walk out from behind the desk.

I feel a handful of eyes follow me. Ugh. That's so annoying. You'd think people have never seen a female cop before. I'm pretty sure a homeless dude, a lawyer, and two handcuffed suspects think I'm worth a roll in the hay. Oh, sure... there's an ego boost. I sigh mentally. Of course, you could put tight jeans on a mannequin and guys will still sprain their necks to check her out.

Kaitlyn appears to be in her later thirties, lots of freckles, and a few faint age lines starting to appear at her mouth and eyes. That, plus her exhausted demeanor, makes me suspect she works a pretty high-stress job. Nothing about her ordinary 'business casual' attire gives away any additional clues of who she is, though I catch a medical symbol on the back face of a laminated ID card hanging around her neck on a cord.

"Kaitlyn?" I ask.

She lifts her head, peering up at me, her expression eager and tinged with worry. "Yes."

I offer a hand. "Detective Maddy Wimsey. You asked to speak with someone in the homicide division?"

"Oh, yes." She stands. "There's a man—"

"Why don't we take this back inside instead of standing around out here?" I smile.

She pauses, makes a 'gee, that was dumb' face, then nods. "Okay."

I escort Kaitlyn back to my work area and gesture at the 'guest' seat beside my desk. She plops down, sets her purse in her lap, and rests her hands on it.

"Would you like some coffee?"

Rick swivels to smile at her. "It's a trap. That stuff will peel paint."

"Yet you still drink it," I say.

He shrugs. "Free makes up for a lot of sin."

Kaitlyn manages a weak smile. "Thank you, I'm okay."

I sit, pull out my notepad, and grab a pen. "All right. Tell me what you wanted to tell me."

She takes a deep breath. "I'm an RN at OHSH."

"That's Olympia Health Services Hospital?" I mutter while jotting it down.

"Yes."

I nod. "Okay. Go on."

"There is another nurse at my hospital, a male nurse named William Johnston, who has been acting really suspicious for months." She pauses, collects her thoughts. "You see, we recently had a patient die unexpectedly under mysterious circumstances, and this guy—William—has always bothered me. Something about him just rubs me the wrong way. You know how you can look at someone and get a chill?"

"Yeah." I nod. "Unfortunately, 'I just know he's a killer' won't exactly hold up in court. Do you have anything a little more firm than a hunch?"

Kaitlyn gazes down at her purse. "Well—and I hope I didn't break the law or anything—but I did snoop around human resources and looked into his work references."

"Not against the law, but grounds for firing, I imagine."

She nods forlornly. "Yeah, probably. Anyway, I couldn't find anything. One number had been disconnected and the other one would only confirm that he had formerly worked there. Typically, when they refuse to say anything at all about what kind of employee a medical worker was, it means there's something wrong but they don't want to talk about it."

"All right..." I jot that down. "And this person who mysteriously died?"

"Patricia Holcomb, aged thirty-five. She'd been under our care for a long time, two years and some months, in what's called a persistent vegetative state. Her prognosis wasn't good. Doctors didn't expect she would ever regain consciousness. Some of her family wanted to pull the plug, but most held out hope. None of them ever caused a scene at the hospital. And I wouldn't imagine any of them would have been able to kill her. Patricia abruptly died in her sleep a few weeks ago. I wasn't on shift at the time, but I've heard rumors going around that she had been given a lethal dose of pancuronium bromide."

Rick swivels toward us. "That sounds kinda familiar."

Kaitlyn lets out a sad sigh. "It's been in the news pertaining to lethal injection. But, it's primarily used as part of surgical anesthesia or to assist with intubation. It's a non-depolarizing muscle relaxant. A high enough dose will paralyze the diaphragm and cause the subject to stop breathing. It's also quite painful when administered."

Rick cringes.

I nod while writing. "Well, we can look into this. Has the family filed any complaint?"

"I don't know." Kaitlyn grimaces. "I'm just an RN, not with administration. I haven't heard anything about a complaint. Also, I have no idea what the doctor told them happened. The way people at OHSH are acting makes me think they know Patricia was murdered but no one wants to say it."

"Too damn many lawyers involved," grumbles Rick. "Hospital is probably more afraid of getting sued than the idea there might be a killer working there."

"Or nothing happened," I say, tapping my pen on the pad and giving him a sideways glance.

My partner shifts his gaze to Kaitlyn in that 'Rick way' of his that tells me he believes her. I'll give the big guy one thing, he *is* good at reading people. "It's worth checking up on at least."

"There's another one, too. Another death, I mean. Suspicious death." Kaitlyn kneads her hands into her purse, her expression frightened and angry in equal parts. "Only last Thursday, this sweet older man, Lyle Winston, passed away under similar circumstances."

"Was he in a vegetative state, too?" asks Rick.

"No. Mr. Winston's kidneys had completely failed. He was fully dialysis dependent. At his advanced age, it was unlikely he'd come up for a transplant list. Even if they could've found a donor, he ran a high risk of not surviving the surgery. He died from acute hypoglycemic shock."

Once I finish guessing how to spell that in my notes, I look up. "Forgive me, Miss Underwood, I'm not entirely sure what that is."

"Low blood sugar, right?" Rick scratches behind his ear. "Friend of mine from high school is diabetic."

"Oh, yeah." I roll my eyes. "Duh. I should've known that."

Kaitlyn nods. "Yes. And it's fine if you call me Kaitlyn. Mr. Winston *did* have very advanced renal disease, and while hypoglycemia is often associated with end-stage renal failure, he had been managing his condition for quite some time without going too far off baseline blood sugar. For him to have such a sudden, unexpected drop into hypoglycemic shock overnight doesn't make sense to me. I'm certain that someone poisoned him with a purposeful insulin overdose that led to his death. The administration isn't even looking into it. All they see is a patient with two nonfunctional kidneys succumbing to hypoglycemia, and they're hand-waving it off as tragic but explainable. Except, none of the other nurses I work with are buying that explanation."

"Is it possible to test for elevated insulin levels?" asked Rick.

Kaitlyn nodded. "Of course. However, I don't think they did."

"All right…" I finish writing a note about insulin testing, then reread what I have so far before looking up at her. "So, this man you suspect is killing people, William Johnston. What can you tell us about him?"

"He's been working at OHSH for seven months. Probably in his forties, salt-and-pepper hair, white guy. Something about the way he looks at people is just *wrong*. I try not to be alone with him, if you know what I mean."

"You are concerned he might assault you?" asks Rick.

"No, not in that way. He doesn't give off any kind of sexual energy whatsoever. It's more an 'I could kill you if I wanted to' stare. The man doesn't have a soul, if you believe in that sort of thing."

I jot down 'creepy, unnerves other nurses' after noting seven months. "Other than the way he makes you feel, is there anything else you've seen or heard that would lead you to suspect his involvement? Something more tangible?"

"He's been spotted going into patient rooms where he isn't assigned. I confronted him once about it, and he blamed his being new and still getting lost around the building. Detective, I grew up with four little brothers, and I'm pretty good at knowing when someone's lying to me. Though, I suppose my apprehension around him could be due to his face."

"What's wrong with his face?" I ask.

"At first, I thought he might've been suffering a condition similar to Bell's palsy, but that only paralyzes half the face. And his face isn't exactly *paralyzed.* Could be, he's just emotionless. Between that, his going into rooms where he doesn't belong, and a strong suspicion that he was forced to resign from his last position… I'm sure there's something going on here. But no one is doing anything about it. That's why I came here."

"Where did he work prior to Olympia Health Services Hospital?" I ask.

Kaitlyn replies, "Saint Bart's," without hesitation.

I jot that down, then hand her one of my cards. "All right. We'll look into it."

"Will you please call me, even if you can't do anything? I'd like to at least know if I should give up hope someone will stop him."

"Sure, I can do that." I smile. "Is there anything else you can think of to tell us that could be helpful?"

She ponders for a moment. "Not right this second, but now that I know you are going to be looking into this, I can quietly ask around among some of the other RNs and see if they'll talk. We're all worried about being dismissed if the administration gets wind of our speaking of it."

Rick sighs and tosses his pen onto his desk. "This one's gonna be interesting."

"All right," I say, standing. "If you learn anything new, please let me know. If there's nothing else, let me walk you out and I'll get started on this right away."

"Thank you!" She springs up. "I'm just glad someone's finally taking this seriously."

It occurs to me that my hair hasn't flopped over my face once while talking to this woman. Darn. This woman's probably right. Or, I've gone off the deep end taking advice from how my hair ends up flopping—or not flopping.

But, hey...

Cops are superstitious creatures.

Chapter Three
The Road to Hell

After returning to my desk from walking Kaitlyn out, I go into the system and look up the two possible victims.

Patricia Holcomb's death certificate shows the cause of death ruled natural, acute brain hypoxia as a result of long term persistent vegetative state. A little internet research tells me that hypoxia means her brain ran out of oxygen and died. That sounds about right for what Kaitlyn described, death via lethal injection so to speak. The drug the nurse accused William of using on her—I check my notes, pancuronium bromide—causes breathing to stop. By logical extension, if someone stops breathing, they're going to run out of oxygen.

One of my odd hunches tells me I am not wasting my time here. Surely, they could detect elevated levels of that drug in a body. Why would they merely list the cause of death as lack of oxygen to the brain? While technically true, that's like saying a murder victim who'd taken a shotgun at close range to the forehead suffered death due to 'brain removal.'

Lyle Winston's paperwork doesn't look quite as suspicious. His cause of death is indicated as acute hypoglycemic shock brought about by complications from kidney failure. Most people looking at this wouldn't have batted an eyelash. Unlike the much younger Patricia, he'd been older, seventy-four according to this certificate.

I call the medical examiner's office. After a game of chicken with the phone menu, I get through to a live person.

"Hi, this is Amanda," says a voice with a faint accent, perhaps Chinese.

"Hey, Amanda. It's Detective Maddy Wimsey. Not sure if you remember me, but we've met a few times in the field. I was hoping you might be able to help me out with a case."

"Sure, what'cha got?" A chair creaks over the line. "And yeah, I remember you. Who could forget that hair? I can't say I envy you when it's humid, although in that regard I guess we're lucky out here."

"Oh, I manage. Just gotta know how to talk to it." I give her the details of the two files. "I have reason to believe these deaths may be more than they appear. Especially Patricia Holcomb's. Why would they list the cause of death as hypoxia?"

"Hmm. Depends on the underlying pathology. Give me a sec to pull these up."

"Thanks."

For a moment or two, the only sound in my ear is the tapping of computer keys while Amanda hums. "Looks like the deceased passed away at a hospital. The doctor there declared the death natural, and no one reported it as suspicious, so it didn't even go through the ME's office. It appears that the hospital conducted the autopsy."

"What are the odds you could reopen that investigation?"

"Pretty low without the family agreeing to an exhumation order... or a judge issuing a warrant for one."

"Damn. What about the other case? Lyle Winston?"

"Hmm. Let me see..." She mumbles to herself unintelligibly while reading for a moment. "That one, yeah, looks like they did send it to us as no next of kin claimed the remains."

Yes! I pump my fist. "Did your autopsy find any evidence of an insulin overdose?"

"No autopsy was performed on him."

"What?! Why not?"

"Because the hospital did one already, and we had no reason to suspect anything out of the ordinary. I guess they assumed an old man pronounced dead by natural causes at a hospital was probably dead, you know, because of natural causes."

"Yeah, well, the road to hell is paved with assumptions, right?" I sigh, clutching a fistful of my hair. "But, I get your point. Nothing raised any red flags, I suppose."

"There was no complaint or appearance of anything untoward," says Amanda.

I let my arm flop on the desk, glaring at the death certificate on the monitor in front of me. "Can you re-test him?"

"Mr. Winston has already been sent off for burial at one of the city's potter's fields. Probably already in the ground at this point."

Argh. So frustrating. My head *almost* makes contact with my keyboard several times. I settle for massaging my sinuses. "Can you try to check him for an insulin overdose? Is a please enough or do I need a warrant?"

"What are you going on?"

"A nurse from the hospital where both of these people died raised some suspicions."

Amanda pauses. "Homicide?"

"Maybe. I'm not entirely sure yet. Was hoping you might be able to give me more information to base an opinion on. The allegation is that Mr. Winston may have been killed with an insulin overdose, and Ms. Holcomb via pancuronium bromide."

"Oh, geez. Okay, I'll see what I can do, but I can't make any promises," says Amanda. "But I can't do anything regarding the woman without involving the family. Her remains were released to the family months ago. Guarantee she's either been buried or cremated by now. At least if they buried her, it's possible to exhume the remains. If she's been cremated, that's a dead end."

I groan.

"Oops, sorry," she says. "I have to quit saying that. It almost always gets that reaction."

Now, I smile. "To a cop, not a problem. To a family member, maybe a problem."

"I'll keep that in mind. Okay, I'll call or email you if I am able to recall Mr. Winston's remains. You know, detective, this would be a lot easier and faster with a warrant."

That time, I do let my forehead crash down on my desk—with my arm in the way. "Yeah, I know."

I hate these chicken-and-egg problems. It's difficult to get a warrant without sufficient probable cause, but the warrant is necessary to obtain enough evidence to establish probable cause in this case. I sit back up. "Thank you, Amanda. Hope you call soon."

"Have a nice day, detective."

After we hang up, I fill Rick in and lean back in the chair and stare at the ceiling.

"Whoa," mutters Rick. "Did I just see that?"

"See what?" I ask, without moving.

"A strand of your hair just reached out and grabbed your coffee cup." Rick, better than most, knows just how freaky I can be... my hair included.

"I think she's trying to cheer me up. Even if the coffee here is ghastly." Now that I think about it, another cup of coffee does sound good about now. I snag the mug and stand.

"So what does your intuition say on this one?" Rick also gets up, mug in hand. "Other than java being a damn fine idea."

I concentrate on the names Patricia Holcomb and Lyle Winston while rubbing my pentacle amulets. A cold sensation swirls around my gut soon after. "Yeah... I think someone killed them."

Chapter Four
Everything

The coffee is brief and crummy.

Hey, police station coffee exists for one reason: caffeine delivery system. Taste is optional. Also, Captain Greer needs something to clean the drains out with every now and then. Rick and I slurp down our coffee while digging a bit into Patricia's life. But, there isn't much in the system about her that would suggest any sort of motive. So, we decide to go talk to Patricia's family to see what we can learn.

Figure the best bet is to start with her parents, Fred and Pam Holcomb. They live in a modest apartment in a relatively inexpensive part of town that's usually home to young people in not terribly great financial shape. An older couple here stands out.

We approach the door together and I ring the

bell mostly because I'm closer on that side.

A moment later, an exhausted-looking woman in her later fifties or maybe early sixties answers. Her grey hair is short and neat, her clothes a utilitarian shirt and jeans. She gives off a pervasive sense of exhaustion and also appears somewhat confused to see people at her door.

"Yes? I think you may have the wrong apartment."

"Mrs. Holcomb?" I ask, holding up a badge. "I'm Detective Madeline Wimsey with the Olympia Police department. This is my partner, Detective Rick Santiago."

"Please, call me Rick." He smiles.

"Detectives?" Mrs. Holcomb blinks. "Now I'm sure you have the wrong apartment. What is this about?"

Rick answers in the same voice he uses to deliver bad news to families. "We received a tip that your daughter's passing may not have been as natural as the hospital documented. It's still too early for us to say if there's anything to this information. We were hoping you might be able to give us some information?"

Mrs. Holcomb's demeanor changes in an instant. She goes from staring up at us like a rabbit stuck on the highway to angry and fierce. "I knew something didn't make sense. It just didn't feel right. Of course I'll talk to you. Please, come in."

She guides us to the kitchen, where two men pore over paperwork. One's about the same age as her, the other in his early thirties with shaggy brown hair. Both look up as we enter.

"This is my husband, Fred, and son Jeremy," says Mrs. Holcomb. "These are detectives asking about Patty."

Fred glances up from whatever form he's reading with an expression like we're from Publisher's Clearing House with a five million dollar check. The son, Jeremy, gives us a 'hey, what's up' sort of nod.

"What's going on?" asks Fred.

Rick re-explains the accusation and the reason for our visit.

"We tried complaining to the hospital, but none of those damned people wanted to hear anything." Fred's face reddens. "And that worthless boyfriend of hers…"

"Easy, Dad." Jeremy puts a hand on his shoulder. "Sorry if he gets short with you. Don't take it personally. He's angry with the insurance companies. My parents had to sell their house a few years ago to pay for Patty's care."

I cringe. "I'm sorry you had to cope with that on top of everything else. Do you have any reason to suspect someone would want to hurt her? Perhaps that 'worthless boyfriend?"

Mrs. Holcomb shakes her head. "Don't mind Fred. He's upset with Shawn for not wanting to sue the hospital."

"Shawn?" I ask.

"Her boyfriend. Shawn, umm…" Mrs. Holcomb

scratches at her eyebrow.

"Thompson, wasn't it?" asks Jeremy.

Mrs. Holcomb snaps her fingers. "Yes."

"So you don't think Shawn—I'm assuming that's the boyfriend—would have wanted to maybe end her suffering?" asks Rick. "Not saying she was suffering, just what he might've been thinking."

Fred grumbles. "No. He shared our hope that she might've gotten better, even if the damn doctors wrote her off."

"Would anyone have a financial incentive to hurt her?" I ask.

The family discusses that for a moment.

"There was a life insurance policy," says Mrs. Holcomb.

"Bah." Fred swats at the paperwork. "Those bastards tried every trick in the book to weasel out of it ever since her accident. We were in the midst of litigation trying to stop them from terminating the policy, but Patty passed away before it ended. The judge ordered them to honor the policy since it was in force at the time of her death. Damn thing barely covered the cost of her funeral. The rest went down the hole of medical bills. My little girl is dead and those sons of bitches are still making money on her corpse."

Jeremy and Mrs. Holcomb both comfort Fred, apparently trying to prevent a screaming rage.

"It's true." Mrs. Holcomb shakes her head with an expression like a schoolteacher who just caught some kid cheating. "From the day of Patty's accident, they'd been trying to cancel the life insurance policy."

"Someone in a persistent vegetative state is going to die," grumbles Fred. "Not a good risk for them."

Rick and I both lean back with forced smiles as Fred erupts in a good four-minute-long F-bomb laced tirade, letting us know in no uncertain terms how he feels about insurance companies. He ends it with, "You should be investigating them. After all the other shit they pulled, it wouldn't surprise me if *they* sent someone to somehow murder my baby girl."

After, an uneasy quiet settles over the kitchen while Fred weeps.

I glance at Rick. The look he's giving me says he shares my opinion of the insurance company hiring a contract killer is just a wee bit far-fetched.

"My apologies for bringing up such painful memories." I flip to a new page in my notepad. "How did she end up in the hospital? Might there be anyone connected to that who could carry a grudge?"

"No." Jeremy shakes his head. "We were at Lyle's place having a party. Lyle Rufolo... he's a friend of mine since, wow... like freshman year of high school. Patty and some of the girls had been goofing around by the pool. Still not sure if she slipped or tried to do something reckless, but she went into the shallow end and hit her head on the bottom of the pool. Knocked herself out and almost drowned."

"She never woke up again," rasps Mrs. Holcomb, on the verge of tears. "They said she'd been deprived of oxygen too long and it caused brain damage. She'd been twenty-six at the time. And no, I don't think Shawn would have hurt her. He told us he'd planned to propose later that summer and asked if we would object to his still marrying her even though she'd ended up in that condition."

Fred shakes his head, but can't manage a word.

"We didn't think it right to make that choice for her." Mrs. Holcomb sighs.

Rick nods. "How did Shawn take her passing?"

"Well..." Mrs. Holcomb looks down. "Fred thought he should've been more upset, but I think the boy made his peace with it a long time ago. I could tell he hurt inside, but he didn't show it much on the outside."

"He's still single," says Jeremy. "And he wasn't married to my sister, so he didn't have anything at all to gain from ending her life."

"Right." I jot that down.

We spend a little while more talking with the family about Patricia's situation. One awkward move at a pool party put her in the hospital for the remainder of her too-short life. The doctors didn't expect she would ever regain consciousness. It's debatable if she even maintained any awareness of being alive. I suppose it's possible that her higher brain functions had been wandering some fantastic dream world while she lay there, but the woman hadn't been comatose. She'd been vegetative. Eyes open, but no reaction whatsoever to external stimuli. I get the feeling that Jeremy didn't have as much hope she'd wake up as the parents, but they're all clearly heartbroken. First at her accident then the death.

"Do you think someone did this on purpose or did the hospital screw up?" blurts Fred.

"It's still too early to say with any certainty." I tap my notepad absentmindedly. "But the tip we received claimed someone did it on purpose. That's why we're here, investigating."

"If you find something, will you tell us?" asks Mrs. Holcomb.

"Of course. As soon as we can do so without compromising the investigation." Rick gives me side eye. I can almost hear him thinking 'assuming there *is* an investigation.'

Yeah. It's not looking good so far. Those people lost everything they had. Their daughter worst of all, but their home, all their savings, years of their life wasted in courts. Though they're in their early sixties, they look ten years older.

If this does turn out to be an actual homicide case, I owe it to them to at least give them some closure.

We thank the family for their time, leave our cards, and head back to the car.

"This one's going to suck," mutters Rick after we get in and close the doors.

"It already does."

"What's your hair say?"

I chuckle. "Nothing yet. But my gut's pretty sure there's something worth looking into here."

"That's what I thought you'd say."

"Yours too?"

"Yep. You know how they say women who live together start having their cycles at the same time? Well, detectives who work together usually start having their guts in sync."

Chuckling, I shake my head. "Right. Lunch?"

"Sure. What'd you have in mind?"

"You pick."

I close my eyes and try opening myself to any hints from the universe. Bad enough I still have the inkling of worry regarding that suicide jump not being a real suicide in my head. Regarding Lyle, life insurance is probably not a motive in his case. It's unlikely he had any, nor do we have any way of confirming one way or the other.

Absent collecting on life insurance, the only possible motive anyone might have had for killing a man in his position would've been from the Medicaid office or the hospital itself, which had been treating him on the cheap as a charity case. Keeping a man with two nonworking kidneys and no insurance alive on constant dialysis for however long he'd have lasted represented a serious financial loss to the hospital. I'm sure their budget department didn't shed many tears over his passing. But as dark as medical finance can be, I strongly doubt a hospital would go to the length of murder to get out from under a patient like Lyle.

At least not *outright* murder. Shady hospitals would've discharged him to a homeless shelter in another city, so he didn't wind up coming right back.

While I'm sure the Olympia Health Services Hospital administration played no active role in Lyle's death, they probably considered it a relief. Then again, medical costs are so damn inflated compared to what things *actually* cost, the money they got from Medicaid to cover him probably did it well enough. So, this is just me being jaded, not really a motive for the hospital to kill him.

For some reason, I can't shake the hunch that the administration covered *something* up. At least, it feels that way. My bet is they're afraid of lawsuits. Possibly someone made a fatal, but accidental, error. But again, Lyle had been homeless before landing in the hospital, with no family or friends around to hire a lawyer. Who did they worry would sue them over it?

What if the hospital realized he'd been murdered and feared any investigation would open a Pandora's box to other cases?

Could there be more victims than Patricia and Lyle?

Chapter Five
Company Line

Rick decides to hit the Fish Tale for lunch. After, we drive across town to Olympia Health Services Hospital.

It takes a little badge waving and a good deal of waiting, but we finally locate a managing nurse by the name of Lydia Navarro. She seems in her late thirties, young for the position, but has a glint in her eyes that tells me she's smart and not easy to intimidate—not that I had any intention of leaning on her. Anyway, she's responsible for managing all the nurses, spending more time in an office than near patients.

"What brings a pair of detectives to my office?" asks Lydia, while shaking our hands.

"We're following up on something that relates to two patients who passed away while here. One, six days ago last Thursday. The other, ten weeks ago. What can you tell me regarding Patricia Holcomb and Lyle Winston?"

Lydia sits back in her chair and clicks around on her computer, spending a minute or four reading, then frowns. "It looks here like both deaths were natural. Not sure why anyone would be investigating them. One poor woman had been very ill for years. Her death was a matter of certainty at some point. Same with Mr. Winston. The man's kidney function had been at nine percent. He required continuous dialysis to survive. I hate to say it, but patients in his situation are at extremely high risk."

"Have you had any issues of nurses behaving strangely, acting odd?" asks Rick. "Any patient complaints?"

"Just the usual... food's too cold. Food's too late. TV doesn't work. Nurse was mean... for making the patient take their medicine. Nurse was rude... for not wanting to kiss the patient."

I grimace. "Some people."

Lydia gives me a 'yeah, seriously' look. "You wouldn't believe the things my nursing staff has to deal with."

"I might. My job puts me in touch with the best and the brightest, too." I hook my thumbs in my jean pockets. "What can you tell me about William Johnston? One of your nurses."

An ever-so-faint twitch in Lydia's left eye tells me something. Exactly what, I'm not sure. She definitely had a reaction to the name, but she's damn good at keeping a poker face, catching herself after less than a second. "He's relatively new." She pivots to the computer and accesses a different program. "Let's see… Hired February twelfth. He works part time, Monday, Wednesday, and Friday from 11:00 p.m. until 5:00 a.m. He's assigned to D wing, general patient care."

"General? As opposed to?" asks Rick.

"Intensive care, critical care, long term, mental ward, post-op recovery, and so on. He assists patients with no particular commonality other than being sick enough to require hospitalization." Lydia reads over something in the file. "There haven't been any disciplinary actions or complaints involving him."

Considering she answered that question before either of us asked it, I assume there have been some complaints or at least suspicions. Then again, the road to hell and all. The Goddess might have sent me a nudge to take this case seriously, but I still need to find actual evidence.

Lydia peers past her screen at us. "May I ask how his name came up?"

"It was mentioned at a prior medical facility where he worked. A patient had died unexpectedly there, too," I say… so fast and smoothly it even surprises me. Yeah, I'm lying out my butt, but for one thing, contrary to what a lot of people think, cops *can* lie to you to trick you into saying stuff. And for another, I think The Goddess just gave me another nudge.

Lydia keeps her cool this time, though a telltale pause makes me wonder what she knows. She doesn't seem *guilty* per se. If I had to caption a picture of her expression, it would be 'shit, that's what I was afraid of.'

"Is William working today?" I ask.

"Today is his day off."

"Do you have his address?"

"I do not, but human resources could help you." She gives me this smile like she just won some game.

An odd hesitation grips me. Normally, in a case like this, we'd try to interview a potential suspect as soon as possible. But… one of my random inklings —that are usually right—makes me not want to do that in this case. Something bad will happen if this guy realizes he's drawn suspicion. I can't put my finger on exactly what the 'something bad' is, but I'll heed my gut for now.

"Fine. Would you mind if we looked at the room where Mr. Winston passed?" I ask.

"I don't see why not." Lydia looks at the screen, taps a few keys. "Mr. Winston was in D3-114 at the time of death. Ms. Holcomb had been in our long term care wing, E5-108. Not sure what you're hoping to see there, but please be mindful if there are any patients in them now."

"Of course." I shake her hand again. "Thank you for your time."

Rick shakes hands with her as well.

I walk out, heading down the hall to the

elevators. "So I'm guessing D3 means third floor, D wing."

"Probably."

Once we're in the elevator, Rick looks over at me. "She held something back."

"Yeah. Noticed the twitch?"

"Yep. And the pause." He sighs. "That woman is towing the company line. She knows more than she's admitting."

"Did you see the way she stared at me when I mentioned why I asked about William?"

He chuckles. "You pulled that straight out of your ass."

"I did." I grin and point to my pendant. "But I had some help… I think."

"No shit?" His playful grin fades to a grimly serious flat line. "Wait. You really think this guy might have killed people, and that nurse who came in with the tip isn't just rattled by a creepy-looking guy?"

"Yeah. I do." I stare at my blurry reflection in the silver-colored doors. "No, I can't prove it… yet. But I think we have a serious issue here."

"Worse than clown killer?"

I groan. Detectives Parrish and Quarrel are working on the worst case of their careers: someone who's murdering random clowns by planting bombs. They have no leads and the attacks have been unpredictable and unrelated to the victims. It's gotten to the point that 'clown' has become a dirty word in the station. "By the Goddess, I hope not."

"That's going to be the case that finally makes Parrish retire." Rick shakes his head. "Worst kind of killer to track down… totally random with no connection to any victim."

The elevator *dings* and the doors slide open.

We head out into a stark white corridor that smells like we crawled into a giant, empty bottle of cleaning solution.

"Back to Ms. Navarro," I say. "I'm thinking she knows, or at least suspects, something is quite wrong with William. That face she made… she had her doubts."

"Which begs the question of why hire him in the first place," says Rick.

"There's been a nationwide shortage of nurses for a long time."

"Oh, I can't imagine why… crappy pay, crappier hours, dealing with people who treat you like shit, political backstabbing from other nurses, elevated risk of contracting diseases, physical injury from lifting patients out of bed… oh, and a grueling education process to even get in the door to begin with. It's a dream job. I can't *imagine* why there'd be a shortage."

I glance at him. "Where'd all that come from?"

"My cousin's a nurse in Boston. He literally unloaded all that shit on Facebook the other day."

"Okay, now I know you have too much time on your hands."

Rick shrugs. "Been a slow few weeks."

Upon locating Lyle's room, I peer in the door.

The instant I do so, a dark feeling spreads over my consciousness. It's unclear whether an angry spirit is glaring back at me, simply stuck here, or if I'm picking up on the negative emotional energy imprinted into the walls at the moment of a violent, unexpected death. Both beds are presently occupied. One by a middle-aged man who's already asleep, the other by an elderly woman in the midst of knitting. So as not to disturb them—and it's not like I'm going to find any forensic evidence here after a week—I keep going to the next room.

The rooms on either side of D3-114 don't give me the same feeling. It is, of course, entirely possible that dozens of people died within a hundred feet of Lyle's room. However, if the ominous energy I sensed in there came from a general sense of death, it would be in the other rooms as well. That it just so happens to be at the place where Lyle passed away under suspicious circumstances is suggestive. I can't rule out that some other person suffered murder in that room. That's the problem with using paranormal information in a police investigation… clues from the other side are open to interpretation and generally don't hold up in court. Besides, the police report forms don't have a checkbox for 'paranormal.'

We head up two floors and into the E wing. Thick, bright yellow stripes running along each wall —as opposed to D-wing's orange—plus loads of floral patterns make this area feel more like a nursing home than a hospital. The room in which

Patricia Holcomb spent the last two years and some months of her life is empty, and it still smells like 'sick person.' The odor isn't particularly bad, merely obvious.

The same dark energy is here as was in Lyle's room, though somewhat more subdued.

"Well?" asks Rick. "What exactly did you hope to find here? It's been a long damn time and I doubt any killer would've left the bottles of drugs they used to murder someone right here on the floor."

I smile. "Not looking for physical evidence. Both rooms feel off. This one weaker. Pretty sure I'm picking up on intention. Emotional energy more than the spirit of a murder victim. Yeah, Rick… I think we're dealing with a killer here. Someone was definitely murdered in these rooms—not simply died. But, I can't take my hunches in front of a judge."

"Great." He sets his hands on his hips, then exhales. "How are we supposed to prove it?"

"That's why we get the big bucks, buddy. Let's push Lydia a little harder."

He nods. "And last I checked, I don't get big bucks."

"Neither do I."

"We should."

"First smart thing you said all day."

He grins. "Better late than never."

***

Lydia Navarro looks up from her desk when we walk in.

"Hello again," I say, smiling. "I just have a few more quick questions if you don't mind."

We get the forced polite smile. "Of course I don't mind. However, I do have a meeting in about twenty minutes."

"I won't be that long. Who was the last hospital employee to see Mr. Winston or Ms. Holcomb alive?"

"Most likely the staff nurse for the evening shift…" She looks at the computer. "Anita Broward in Ms. Holcomb's case." She taps a few buttons. "And John Riley for Mr. Winston."

I jot those names down. "Any visitors on the day they died?"

"You'd have to ask the floor nurses for details like that. I can tell you what nurse was on staff at any given day, but the details of patients or visitors on that level isn't something I'd know about."

"All right." I nod. "And you've heard nothing out of the ordinary regarding either of those patients, or any nurses who may have been around those patients?"

She shakes her head. "I'm sorry, detective. If anything unusual did occur, it was not brought to my attention."

Rick and I exchange a glance. We often joke that we've figured out a way to manage rock paper scissors with a series of blinks, deciding to push harder or not. He gives me the back off look. Yeah,

Rick's right. We don't have any grounds to go into attack mode… yet.

"Understood. Thank you again for your time. If anything does come to your attention, please call us."

"Of course, detective." Lydia smiles. "Have a pleasant day."

Reluctantly, I walk out of her office.

"Damn, you have any cash on you? We were here for like forty-five minutes. Parking's gonna be at least sixty bucks for that long."

I smirk. "We're using an official vehicle. We don't pay to park."

"Ehh, Wims, this one's under your skin already? You're supposed to laugh, not hit me with logic."

"Sorry." I fake laugh.

"She wants us to go away," says Rick, as we turn a corner and head down a short corridor toward one of the exits. "Far away."

"I'm pretty sure this guy is going to kill again, especially with an administration covering for him."

"Does that make them an accomplice?"

"You'd have an easier time proving Hoffa dead." I shove the door out of my way and head to the sedan.

"Wims, it's 2019. There's no way that man's alive anymore. Hell, he's dead simply from old age."

I shrug and open the driver's side door. "Good point. And that's a good sign."

"What is?"

"You just proved Jimmy Hoffa's dead without much trouble." I fall into the seat. "Let's hope proving there's a killer at work here is just as easy."

"Doubt it," says Rick.

I sigh. "I know. I'm just trying to stay positive."

"Last I checked, my name's not Dr. Phil," says Rick. "This is the real world, with real killers. Staying positive isn't part of the job description. Catching killers is, and sometimes it ain't easy."

"Remind me not to call you when I need some picking up."

"It's called tough love, Wims. Now, do you want a vanilla iced latte or not?"

"I want a vanilla iced latte."

He grins. "Then let's go."

Chapter Six
The Blind Crow

Upon returning to my desk, I shift into research mode hoping that something in the victims' backgrounds might clue me in on a potential killer by virtue of motive.

According to what I got from her parents, Patricia Holcomb had last been employed as a customer service rep for an outsourcing company providing headcount for other companies that didn't want to manage or hire an internal support team. Fortunately, Patty and her mother had been close, so she called all the time to talk about her life. Aside from arguments over who took whose lunch out of the break room fridge, that doesn't sound like the kind of job that could make someone a target for murder. They're also unrelated to the injury that put her in the hospital. She'd hurt herself at a pool on a day off. Sad to think about how hopeful her family was she'd get better. Computers are awesome for research, but they have a downside: distraction. I waste some time reading articles about persistent vegetative states and their recovery rates... before I catch myself and go back to checking up on her past.

She didn't have any enemies that are obvious from the information available to me online or from anything her parents and brother mentioned. No kids, no unusual amounts of debt... just an ordinary twenty-six-year-old woman who wound up dead as a not-so-ordinary thirty-five-year-old critical care patient.

I do a little better upon looking into the second possible victim of homicide, Lyle Winston. His life reads like a rollercoaster. And by reads, I'm talking about what I'm able to discern from his social security history. Based on past employment, I suspected he didn't start with much. No evidence that he went to college, either. But in his late twenties, he moved out of Tacoma and to Bellevue. I do a quick address search and see it's the nice part of Bellevue. In his fifties, he filed for bankruptcy, which is about when his address started having gaps in the record.

But it isn't all that much to go on. I call Kaitlyn Underwood—the nurse who showed up to tell us about this case—and ask her if she can think of anyone who might have known him, visited, or spoken with him regularly. She asks me to hang on, and a few minutes later, I'm speaking to another nurse named Tatianna, who'd formed a friendship with the old guy.

Apparently, Lyle could be a talker, especially since he couldn't get out of bed too well with all the hoses and whatnot. She relays to me things he'd shared with her over the past year or so. He'd started off dirt poor, spent many decades doing quite well for himself, then lost everything and ended up on the street. Apparently, old Lyle had a bit of a gambling issue and that extended to a habit of risky stock investments that ultimately bit him square in the ass, wiping out whatever retirement savings he hadn't gambled away in Vegas.

I do find some legal proceedings in public record with his name, mostly involving civil suits. A few hours skimming court transcripts suggests someone might have had a motive for revenge. A man named Antoine Shemp sued him over and over again throughout the years. There's even a criminal case where the man had been convicted of assault with a deadly weapon for an attack on Lyle in 1972. I dig up those court transcripts. Apparently, the then-thirty-one-year-old Lyle Winston had edged Shemp out of the company they co-founded by tricking him into agreeing to a buyout. Two months later, the new board of directors dismissed Shemp, but kept Lyle on.

I sit back and consider the data I've collected. In my book, kicking in the door of a person's home, then charging inside while swinging an axe is more like attempted murder than assault with a deadly weapon, but maybe the DA's office felt bad for the guy. Who knows? The case is old and there aren't too many records. Shemp served a little over seven years before being paroled. His record remained clean after that for the most part. Recently, he's been picked up a handful of times for public intoxication and vagrancy.

"Hey, Rick. Look at this. I found a former business associate named Antoine Shemp who might have had a motive."

His chair creaks. "What, Shemp like one of the Three Stooges?"

"False stooge," says Parrish from his desk. "Shemp was a fake. The true third stooge was Curlee."

"Excuse me a moment." Rick walks over to Parrish's desk, and the two men get into a debate about the legitimacy of comedians from like the 1930s or whatever. Not much I can do but stand there in absolute disbelief. Though, the sound of soft weeping coming from Quarrel's desk is mildly alarming. Pretty sure he's not upset about stooges, fake or otherwise. Though, speaking of fake, I'm sure he's pretend crying over his frustration about the clown case.

Eventually, Rick and Parrish agree to disagree. My partner walks back, muttering, and leans past my shoulder to check out the info I have on Shemp. His dangling necktie and my hair get into a fight. He makes a mildly annoyed face like he thinks I'm pulling on his tie, but doesn't look down before flipping it up over his shoulder. I'm not entirely sure, but I think my hair is proud of itself for 'winning.'

Parrish abruptly tromps down the hall to one of the small conference rooms.

"Okay, that happened forty-six years ago." Rick stands out of his lean and gestures at my monitor before pulling his tie back down in front of his chest.

"Except he didn't give up. Even before he got out of prison, Shemp kept firing off a barrage of lawsuits and legal motions. Didn't lay off that until almost five years ago when Winston wound up homeless."

"Kinda thin, don't ya think?" Rick scratches behind his ear.

"Yeah. I realize It's not much, but it's the only thing I can come up with aside from a serial killer who chooses his victims randomly. Someone with no connection whatsoever to the victims. Feel like talking to the guy? Maybe he knows someone else who wouldn't be so hesitant."

Rick rubs his chin. "Why would anyone wait until Winston's an elderly, brittle shell of a home-less guy sitting in the hospital with two failed kidneys? He'd been on the street a while before that. They could've gotten their revenge at any time. Hell, leaving him alive at that point would've been more revenge than a quick death."

I sigh, and it does feel like a massive reach.

"You're right."

"Look, if all other leads dry out, we can revisit this one. Might be time to talk to William Johnston. Who knows, maybe we can get a confession out of him. Stranger things have occurred."

Something pulls my hair... and I'm pretty sure that something is the Goddess. Or something damn close to the Goddess. It would be worthless for me to turn to see if someone is standing behind me, tugging my locks. I know there's no one there. And I also know there's something important I need to know. It's something I'd been feeling since getting this case and I hadn't put words to, but the word came now.

"No, Rick. Not yet. He's a flight risk. Or a suicide risk. Or one of us will get hurt if we move too fast on him. Or something. I just know that if we talk to him now, we may never get a chance to talk to him again."

"And you know this how?"

"Just trust me."

"A few seconds ago, I saw you wince in pain... did that have anything to do with it?"

"Yes."

"Fine. We hold off talking to him. So where does that leave us?"

"We collect enough evidence to detain him before we let him know he's under suspicion."

"We need a search warrant to collect any evidence at the hospital."

I smile; after all, I felt the equivalent of gentle

stroking along one side of my head. "Leave that to me. Hmm. Speaking of evidence, just to be absolutely sure we're not barking up the wrong tree with Johnston, why don't we find Shemp? Eliminate him as a suspect so we're certain we're not wasting time chasing that nurse around."

"All Right. But you're driving."

***

Antoine Shemp doesn't have a permanent address that I can find.

However, a little old-fashioned police work— running around with a photograph and asking if anyone knows this man—eventually leads to a tip from a guy named Jambalaya that Antoine is usually holed up at a bar named The Blind Crow.

Beats driving all over the place, so we head there.

"I still think we should be looking at the insurance company or the hospital," says Rick. "And I'm being somewhat cynical here, but also a little serious. Lyle Winston was a huge financial burden. The only party who truly gained from his death is whoever no longer has to cover the cost of his hospitalization and care."

I take the next left, turning onto the street where the bar is located. "That's more than somewhat cynical. Doesn't feel right. He'd been at that hospital for nine months already. If they had any intention of doing something horrible, they would've done it a while ago."

"Perhaps they had been waiting for a better opportunity and once they had a freak-a-deak nurse on staff, he turned into a scapegoat?"

"What are you saying? The hospital administration sent Kaitlyn to get us going on an investigation just to pin a murder that bureaucrats orchestrated on an innocent but odd nurse?" I pull over near the bar, surprisingly finding a parking spot not *too* far away.

"It does sound rather implausible when you put it that way. But remember Lydia Navarro. That woman basically lied straight to our faces to protect the hospital."

"True." I cut the engine. "Though, I suspect she is more worried about lawsuits than criminal charges. And, I've got a feeling."

"Once more, with feeling," mutters Rick.

I chuckle and get out.

"The bar looked like any other dive bar I'd ever been in, but I had a feeling that whatever waited for me inside this place would be far from usual," says Rick in his best noir voice.

"You watch far too many old movies." Shaking my head, I walk down the sidewalk to the door.

The Blind Crow really does look like a dive bar. I say 'looks like' because it's difficult to tell if it actually is a shithole or if it's one of those hipster places that attempts to look like a dump on purpose. That whole rustic/worn aesthetic is something I still don't understand. Why would anyone want to buy a brand new piece of furniture made to resemble a piece of rotting wood left in a compost heap from the forties? B.B. King leaks from an old jukebox in the back on the far side of a beat-up pool table with sticks so warped they'd probably return if thrown— like boomerangs.

At least the place doesn't stink. If you don't count saturated fruitiness from a legion of vape inhalers going full blast for years inside a room with poor ventilation.

Naturally, all the guys in the place stop what they're doing and look at me when we walk in. This isn't the sort of bar people like me go to. One, I'm a woman. Two, I'm *way* too pale, and three, I'm about thirty years too young. Oh, and the badge on my belt is probably not making me any friends.

"Beer's a little more to your likin' at Hanrahan's couple blocks that way," says the bartender. He's an older black gentleman, probably not quite seventy yet. Reedy thin, with a strong hint of territorial defensiveness in his eyes, but also warmth. I get the feeling he's playing a character more than really trying to shoo me off. Maybe he thinks someone else here will be trouble for me, or he's just putting on a show for the regulars.

"There he is," mutters Rick. "End of the bar."

The dozen or so guys in the room keep watching me as I approach the bartender. "Not here to drink. Thanks for the tip, but when I'm in the mood to get shit-faced, I prefer Riordan's Pub. Hanrahan's has crappy fights."

He chuckles, clearly done with the 'you've gone

into the wrong bar' attitude. "Well, then miss. What can I do for you?"

"Detective, actually. With homicide. Not here to rattle anyone's cage." I nod toward Shemp. "Just need a moment of his time."

The bartender makes a 'be my guest' gesture.

Rick nods in acknowledgment at a few of the other guys, none of whom have yet made a sound since we entered. They don't nod back at him.

Shemp looks and smells well into pickled. I suppose with it being nearly six in the afternoon, it's only *slightly* early for someone to reach this level of inebriation. Then again, I have the feeling this guy is used to seeing vapor trails by noon.

"Mr. Shemp?" I ask.

Rick stifles a snicker.

"Ya, what you want?" He un-drapes himself from the bar and nearly wobbles backward off his stool.

Yikes. He's maybe eighty pounds. If he keeps drinking like this, it won't be long before he and Winston are face to face again, so to speak. "We're here about Lyle Winston."

Shemp appears to sober up a little, narrowing his eyes at me. "What about the son of a bitch?"

My hair shrinks behind me to avoid the assault of alcohol fumes blasting me in the face.

"Mr. Winston passed away recently. We understand you two once worked together," says Rick.

"The ol' cheating shit is dead?" Shemp leans

back and cackles.

I lunge forward to grab him when he begins to fall off the stool again. Rick gets his other arm and we pull the man upright, holding on for a moment until he stops laughing.

"That's correct," I say.

"Well then, little lady…" He smacks the bar twice, emitting a noise part balloon losing air, part giggle. "If you find out who did it, you let me know so I can shake their hand."

Rick raises an eyebrow. "We haven't mentioned how Mr. Winston died."

"Heh, yeah, yeah." Shemp grins, picks up his empty glass, then sighs at it. "You two wouldn't be here to talk ta me if ol' Lyle kicked the bucket all peaceful like in his sleep. I left a paper trail long enough to wrap around the Earth two times. So, I figure you two thinkin' I might've helped Lyle shuffle off 'dat mortal coil."

"We're just following up on any possible leads." Rick smiles.

Shemp wags the glass at the bartender. "Hey, Larry. How 'bout it, huh?"

"You got the back room yet to sweep," says the bartender, evidently, Larry.

"I'll get to it later."

Larry gives us a look that says 'later never comes.'

The old guy makes a sour face at the glass, then shifts to face us. "My abode ain't exactly what ya would call livin' uptown. I'm half tempted ta tell you two I did it just for a decent bed and hot meal, but you'd kick me out in a couple hours when I didn't know nothin'. Happy the ol' weasel finally got what's comin' to him, but ain't my doin'."

Rick starts talking to him about the reasons behind his feelings toward Mr. Winston while I drift off for a chat with the bartender.

"What can you tell me about Mr. Shemp over there?" I ask in a low voice.

"Not much. Guy's here pretty much all day every day. Open to close. Sometimes I let him sleep in the back room."

"Sometimes?" I ask.

"As long as he's not in one of his moods."

"He gets violent?"

"Ehh, I can see where you'd make that assumption, but not like that. Shouts and yells a lot. Might knock over glasses or chairs. Wouldn't attack a person, though. Feel bad for the man, but when he gets like that, no tellin' that he won't break into the cabinets and drink himself straight to death."

"Last week, Thursday, do you remember if you let him sleep here?"

"I do. Sure as seein' you now. He's been havin' a good couple o' weeks."

Since I'm almost totally confident there is no possible way Shemp could get his hands on pancuronium bromide or insulin, much less sneak into a hospital after visiting hours undetected, I don't bother pressing Larry. Hell, if Shemp had been in Lyle's hospital room when he died, the area would *still* smell like cheap scotch. He also doesn't seem to be lying.

Mr. Shemp bursts into laughter. He and Rick start spouting off the weirdest things. It takes me a moment to realize they must be quoting *The Three Stooges.* Guess with a name like that poor man's got, he's used to hearing it.

"Thanks," I say to Larry, then wander a step or two away and wait for Rick.

The rest of the patrons have—mostly—stopped staring at me, though none have resumed any conversations yet. Some old R&B music comes from the jukebox that makes me feel like I've gone back in time to the Fifties, but I don't recognize it.

Eventually, Rick pats Shemp on the shoulder and walks over to me. Pretty sure the last fifteen minutes or so of their talk had nothing to do with the investigation. We make our way out, and as the door swings shut behind us, the din of people talking picks up like a soundtrack taken off pause.

"Wow, that was surreal," I mutter.

"Ehh, don't read into it too much. That's an old guy's bar. We're not old, and we've got badges."

"Right." I hop in the car, shut the door, and sigh. Not to be *too* critical of the poor man, but I can still smell him.

Rick lowers himself in. "I dunno about you, but I'm looking forward to going home."

"Hot date with the heavy bag tonight?" I start the engine, smiling at him.

"Nah. *X-Files* marathon."

"You live on the edge."

"Totally." He closes his eyes.

As soon as traffic lets me, I pull into the street and accelerate. "Shemp's not involved."

"I agree. Which puts us back at square one."

"Square two. We still have that nurse the nurse mentioned that the other nurses have been complaining about. Or are you still nursing your doubts?"

I sigh.

He snickers.

Chapter Seven
Personal Issues

One perk about being a detective is not having to wear a uniform.

That lets me skip the locker room most days since I don't have to change upon going off-duty. After we do our end of day stuff, mostly case progress reports, I don't need to change before leaving. It's a little past the end of our official hours, but those are just for show. Pretty sure any detective who can 'put in their eight and go home' is either doing something wrong or works for a precinct where a kid shoplifting a pack of gum is a citywide scandal.

And, since I don't work in Mayberry, my nice little scheduled hours are pretty much there for administrative purposes. No, it doesn't bother me. I'm helping the citizens of my community. Also,

I'm not here purely for the paycheck. I don't think anyone who does this job is. *Way* too much bullshit to deal with, both paperwork wise and emotionally. Ever since Caius and I got serious, I didn't really need to even keep working at all. He makes plenty enough for me to be a stay-at-home girlfriend. Soon to be a stay-at-home wife. Wow, I still can't believe he finally proposed.

That puts a giant grin on my face as I head off toward the parking lot.

A uniformed officer coming the other way down the hall makes the kind of eye contact with me that says he wants to talk. He looks concerned, and despite being around my age—mid-thirties—his demeanor is more like that of a boy about to ask a teacher for help.

I slow as we draw closer, tilting my head in response, wordlessly asking 'can I help you?'

"Detective Wimsey?" asks the cop, Lovell, D. according to his nameplate. Blue stripes on his sleeve tell me he's a shift supervisor, also a sergeant. Not a rookie.

"Yeah, that's me." I smile.

"Can we have a quick chat? Perhaps somewhere a little quieter?"

What I said before about a kid asking a teacher for help? Dial that back. It would be more accurate to say he's giving off vibes like a guy about to tell his doctor he can't get it up. He's part embarrassed, part desperate… and for some reason, thinks I'm the one who can fix things. I don't think Parrish told anyone about the potion I made for when his son had that poison ivy issue. However, somehow, I think I've become the station's resident witch doctor.

Maybe I should get a little cabin out in the woods somewhere so formerly virile young men can risk their lives battling the forces of nature to reach me and beg for a magic potion. Okay, I shouldn't think about that because it's going to make me laugh, and this man looks far too serious and vulnerable.

"Sure."

Officer Lovell doesn't say much else until after we duck into the nearest interrogation room for some privacy. "Thanks for talking to me. I've been having an issue at home that I... can't really explain."

"That can often happen to men in high-stress jobs. I can think of a few herbal teas that might help you rise to the occasion."

"There—" He pauses, blinking at me. "Oh... no. That's working just fine." Officer Lovell blushes a little, chuckles, then goes serious again. "It's something else."

This should be good, whatever it is. "What's the issue then?"

He lets out a long sigh. "Promise me you won't laugh or think I'm crazy?"

"Most everyone here already thinks I'm weird." I point at my pentacle amulets.

"That's why I thought you might be able to

help. Look, there's something happening at my house. At first, I didn't take it seriously... but I *saw* something I can't explain."

My sense of humor takes a back seat to concern, mostly from the fear in the man's expression. "Something supernatural?"

He looks at the windows like a drug dealer checking for cops, then mutters, "Yeah. At least, that's what I think. This is going to sound silly, but I think my house is being haunted."

"That doesn't sound silly to me," I say, completely serious. "I've seen plenty of things most people would call bullshit on."

"Especially cops. Anyone gets wind of this, I'll be peeling Ghost Busters stickers off my stuff for the rest of my career."

"Well, you better talk fast before someone notices us hanging out in a dark interrogation room." I smile. "Your wife might not be too happy when *those* rumors get started."

He shakes his head dismissively. "Nah. Brianna's not the jealous type. Anyway... so the kids were telling me about a monster. I didn't take it seriously at all, but then I saw something that completely shut my brain down. Skye, my daughter, woke up screaming in the middle of the night a few days ago. When I checked on her, she's curled up against the headboard of her bed, hiding behind her pillow and screaming." He rubs his forehead. "Okay, this next part is going to sound completely unhinged, but I swear it's the truth. In the corner of her room, I saw like a column of black smoke with glowing eyes. And the damn thing growled at me."

Shit. That's not good. "What did you do?"

"I freakin' grabbed Skye and ran down the hall to our bedroom. Whatever it was didn't follow us, and had vanished by the time I checked back a few hours later. But that's not the worst of it. The next night, something dragged my son Marcus straight out of his bed. Splat, right on the floor. I mean, he like legit got hurt. I don't know what to do, Maddy. My kids are having nightmares and neither will sleep in their own rooms. My kids are going to wind up in therapy if whatever this thing is doesn't hurt them worse. Anyway, everyone at the station keeps talking about how you're spoo—I mean into stuff they don't understand. Is there anything you can think of that I can do?"

I smile. "I've been called much worse than spooky. My first question for you is what changed?"

He blinks. "Pardon?"

"When did your daughter start having nightmares?"

"Umm. About three weeks ago."

"Okay. What changed three weeks ago?"

"I'm still not sure I understand what you're asking me."

"Did you bring anything new into the house that hadn't been there before? Furniture? Vase? Old jewelry box? Ancient mummy you picked up at a garage sale?"

He stares at me for a few seconds before realizing the last one is a joke, then laughs. "Umm. Nothing I can think of. Maybe my wife might know. Speaking of which, the thing even tried to kill her."

"How?"

"Pushed her down the basement stairs. Maddy, what the hell is this thing?"

I tap my teeth. "Could be an old ghost or perhaps a dark spirit... something most people today would call a demon. It's exceptionally rare for them to simply wander by and decide to move into a house. Yeah, definitely ask Brianna if she brought any objects home recently, specifically around the time your daughter started having bad dreams."

"Okay. I can do that. But what if she didn't bring anything home? She's not really into antiques or anything."

"I can check it out sometime if you don't mind inviting a witch into your home." I put on my most innocent smile.

"How about Friday after work?"

"Sure. That's fine... as long as nothing blows up."

The color runs out of his cheeks.

"Oh, no. I didn't mean literally explode. Your house is fine. I meant metaphorically blow up. If I don't get stuck at a crime scene, I'll see you Friday."

Officer Lovell nearly passes out, he exhales so

hard. Smiling, he takes out a business card, scribbles his home address and number on the back, and hands it to me. "Thanks, detective. I really appreciate it."

"One thing you can do if it gives you trouble before Friday, face it down and tell it that it has no power here and it needs to leave."

He fidgets. "Don't you have to be like a priest or something for that? My wife and I aren't super religious. I mean, we believe in God, but we haven't been to church in... gosh, I have no idea."

I chuckle. "It doesn't make a difference. Paradoxically, less belief in the supernatural tends to protect people more from these things. You're a cop. Just think of it as another punk who just robbed a gas station."

"Yeah, but I can tase the shit out of a punk." He chuckles.

"You might not want to try that here." I raise a finger. "Electricity and electromagnetic energy can make them stronger. Plus the darts would go right through it and could hit someone."

Officer Lovell nods. "Right. So just order it to leave, and that will work?"

"The more you believe it will work, the better the chances of it working." I write my personal cell number on one of my cards and give it to him. "If things get way out of hand before Friday, let me know and I'll get over there as fast as I can."

"Thanks."

"No problem. Stay safe out there."

He salutes me with the card. "You too, detective."

I poke my head out of the interrogation room to make sure no one is watching, then duck out. The last thing I need are *more* rumors starting about 'the wild redhead.'

Chapter Eight
Premonitions

Caius and I go out on a double date with my friend Isabelle and her husband Owen.

I'm rocking a sheer sapphire blue satin gown split down one side, and matching heels. Of course, those shoes are mostly to carry my butt from the car to the table and back. For most of the night, they'll be set off to the side.

My fiancée—still feels weird to call him that—picked a nice steakhouse type place. I wouldn't necessarily call it 'upper end,' but it's no chain. That is one thing I adore about him. For the money his family has, he doesn't flaunt it at all. I'm sure they wouldn't rank even within the top thousand richest people in the country, but they're in no danger of ever going broke. At least not without some extremely stupid investment decisions.

He's decked himself out in one of his nice black suits with a dark red brocade vest, frilled ascot and sleeves. It's not *quite* Victorian looking. Aside from the fancy bits, the rest of the outfit looks contemporary. Then again, as far as I'm concerned, Caius could wear a trash can with a head hole cut out of it and still be smoldering.

Isabelle showed up in a nice normal cream-colored dress, while Owen decided the button-down shirt with jeans combination ought to work. In truth, Caius and I somewhat overdressed and he somewhat under-dressed. Izzy hit the bull's eye, at least going by what everyone else in here is wearing.

For the hour or two I'm here with people as close as family to me, it's possible to stuff all the job drama in a box and keep it out of sight. Possible isn't the same as easy, though. That is one thing I could do without regarding my job—the constant sense that I'm being callous by doing anything other than working on a case when there's the potential of an active killer out there. That whole 'who am I to sit here having fun with friends while someone could die' guilt is a real pain in the ass.

However, tonight, that feeling isn't as strong as it usually is, so I cross my fingers and hope it's a whisper from The Goddess that I'm occasionally allowed to enjoy myself and nothing bad will happen for me being here.

I drift out of my guilty mental wanderings soon after the waiter brings the salads over. Izzy's in the midst of telling Caius (and me, despite my zoning out) that Noah—that's her three-year-old son, who's spending the night at his grandmother's—is going to his first birthday party on Monday.

"It's so adorable that he's made a friend. They live next door to us," says Isabelle, still holding her first forkful of salad she has yet to bite. It's been like five minutes.

Owen pauses in his project to singlehandedly annihilate the entire basket of breadsticks that came out with the salads, and grins. "Yeah, those two are going to get into a lot of trouble when they get older. I can just picture Noah rigging a clothesline or something so they can zip-line across the space between the houses." He swallows the wad of bread he'd been talking past. "Their bedroom windows face each other, not that either of them realize it yet."

"Mason's mother even hired a clown for the party," chirps Isabelle before eating her salad… finally.

A nasty chill runs down my back the moment the C-word leaves her lips. The frigidity settles in my stomach like an angry snake hiding in a rabbit burrow. In an instant, I'm reminded of how I felt just prior to my grandfather's death… that same terrible coldness. A wave of guilt passes over me again at his death, and once again I let it go. I have to.

And yeah, like others at the station, even I've started thinking about it like the C-word. 'Clown' has become the dirtiest of swears at work. I could scream the *other* C-word and it probably wouldn't get half as many angry glares. Of course, that makes me think about the homicide investigation that's been driving Parrish and Quarrel crazy for the past two months. Crazy enough that they've taken to walking into random empty rooms and just scream- ing to release tension. We're up to nine separate attacks, three of which ended in death for unfortu- nate clowns. All the victims are freelance 'clowns for hire' who typically work the birthday party circuit for little kids. Three attacks happened in Seattle, so the case has gone interdepartmental. BATF is involved as well as the FBI. The feds haven't 'pulled jurisdiction' on us yet, more like they're acting in an advisory capacity. I'm sure they'll take the reins if this guy strikes out of state. Also, I'm fairly certain that Parrish and Quarrel are offering sacrifices to dark gods in hopes the FBI will take the case away from them.

This would be the first time in recorded history the local cops *want* the feds to pull rank.

I think Parrish even offered to buy the whole federal squad a steak dinner if they took over.

Still, it's not a good sign that I felt a chill as soon as she said clown.

"Izzy, it might not be a great idea to let Noah go to that party. Or Mason. Or any child really."

"Aww, clowns aren't that scary," says Isabelle with a smile. She loads her fork up with more salad that she's probably going to hold without biting for another five minutes. "You've had a thing about clowns ever since we were in... what was it, sixth grade?"

"You still haven't read *It*, have you?" I ask.

"Read what?"

"*It.*"

Isabelle looks around. "What are you talking about?"

Caius covers his mouth to hold in a laugh.

I sigh. "The book titled *It.*"

"Oh!" She rolls her eyes. "Duh. No. I don't do horror. And I especially don't do *books* that give you nightmares."

Owen peers up at me from his reenactment of a starving horse running amok at an all-you-can-eat buffet. "How the heck does anyone get a nightmare from a book anyway? Books aren't scary. Now movies..."

"That just means you lack imagination." I wink, then give Isabelle a serious look. "Not kidding. Got a weird feeling. Who is the clown?"

"No idea. Mason's mother made the arrangements." She looks at Owen. "What was her name again?"

"Mrren," mutters Owen past a mouthful of romaine and bread.

"Lauren! That's right." Isabelle, surprisingly, eats that mouthful of salad before fishing around her purse for her phone. "So why are you hung up on clowns?"

Caius holds up a hand. "Unless you wish to

spend the rest of tonight talking about police matters, I suggest you simply accept there's an issue."

"Hah. It's not quite that bad. Not even my case. This is mostly me getting a *feeling.*"

"Oh." Caius, picking up on my meaning, looks at the two of them with the utmost sense of urgency in his face. "You should take this seriously."

"I am!" Isabelle finds her phone, yanking it out of her disorganized purse with all the fanfare of King Arthur drawing Excalibur. "Sec."

Owen chases a few stray scraps of lettuce around his salad bowl while Caius and I continue eating ours like ordinary people. My best friend's husband isn't necessarily the sort of guy you simply can't take anywhere nice. He was in the Army for a couple years and something about it made him eat ridiculously fast when he doesn't focus on slowing down. I vaguely remember him telling us a story about this time he found out he had to be somewhere in two minutes right after he sat down to have dinner—and ate an entire (large) plate of food in roughly thirty seconds.

Ugh. My stomach hurts merely thinking about that.

Isabelle has a brief conversation with her neighbor about the clown. To avoid causing unnecessary alarm, she says her friend is looking for a clown and wanted his contact information. She nods, pulls a pen out of her purse, and copies a phone number plus website down on one of the paper drink napkins. "Thanks! Uh huh. Yeah. No problem.

Yeah, we're still on for shopping tomorrow. At a restaurant now. Kinda gotta go. Okay. See you." She hangs up and pushes the napkin over. "The guy's name is Michael Alvarez."

To save time, I take a photo of the napkin and send it to Parrish. I still have his contact info in my personal cell since he used to be my training partner back when I first made detective. He's basically like an older brother to me.

"Excuse me a minute," I say, stand, and head for the ladies' room—or at least the little secluded hallway right outside it. Once away from the din of the restaurant, I call him.

"Geez, Wims. You still don't have a social life, do you?" asks Ed, by way of answering.

"Actually, I'm in the middle of said social life."

"Oh?"

"At Griffin's."

"Ahh. That's right. I keep forgetting you're dating a rich guy."

I smirk, not that he can see it. "Caius isn't rich. And this place isn't that expensive."

"Forty bucks for a steak is expensive. Anyway, what's up with this napkin? Who's Michael Alvarez?"

"He's a c-word. My friend's neighbor hired this guy to do a party for her son this coming Monday. A chill hit me as soon as she said the word that which cannot be named. The only other time I've ever felt a chill like that, my grandfather died. I was on the phone with Gram, and she said he'd gone out for a ride. A chill hit me, but I didn't know what that meant. An hour later, he's dead. Fell off the stupid horse and broke his neck."

My voice catches in my throat. It makes no sense to feel guilty. I'd only been thirteen at the time. How could I have known The Goddess or whatever power of the universe tried to warn me to tell him not to ride that horse at that time?

"Oh, shit. I'm sorry. So you think this is the guy we're after?"

"Not exactly."

"Then what? Maybe some kinda rival thing, like eliminate the competition?"

I shake my head in the empty hallway. "The only explanation for the feeling I got is if Isabelle or Noah are going to be hurt at the party. I wouldn't get this jolt for a total stranger. Your suspect has been planting bombs to kill clowns. Me getting that feeling makes me think Mr. Alvarez may unknowingly bring an explosive device to the party, and that device is going to hurt people I care about."

"Shit… do you think this is serious?"

"As serious as any of the 'woo-woo stuff' gets." That's his term for all things paranormal.

"All right. So this party is Monday?"

"Yep. Maybe set up a stakeout on the Alvarez guy's home or office… wherever he keeps his props and stuff. Might catch the suspect planting the bomb. If nothing happens, please stop the guy before he gets to the party on Monday and search his car."

"I'll see what I can do. Thanks for the head's up. I'll take any help we can get."

"Even witchy help?"

"Especially witchy help." He chuckles. "You should get back to your table before your friends think you've gone off to the station."

"Yeah. Thanks, Ed. Be careful."

"Will do."

I hurry back to the table. Our dinners have already arrived. My sirloin looks amazing, even if I can barely see any meat under the mushrooms and onions piled onto it.

"Everything okay?" asks Isabelle.

"I think so. Hard to say."

Caius smiles over his wine at her. "You'll have to give her some leeway. The premonition thing is new for her."

I crack up laughing with a bit of steak inches from my teeth, then elbow him in the side. The guy says something randomly once that turns out to be prophetic and all of a sudden he's the expert. "Sorry for edging in on your territory."

"Oh? You're like prophetic or something?" asks Owen. "When did that start? Some spell you cast?"

"It wasn't actually a prediction of the future." Caius takes a sip and sets his glass down. "Ever have a random thought come out of nowhere? A bit like that, only it turned out to be meaningful. Maddy was frustrated about a case and I randomly thought of the word 'Wexford.' Turned out to be the name of the street where her suspect would strike next."

"Neat." Owen grins.

"Now you just have to tune that into the lottery or something," says Isabelle in an obviously joking tone. She knows we wouldn't use magic for personal gain.

The blowback could be too severe. Besides, we're doing okay.

Luck, on the other hand, is a lot less dangerous to ask for. Something tells me Caius's mother, Abigail, or maybe her mother, worked one heck of a luck spell a while ago. It's done well for the Craven family, and it's spilled over onto me. After all, I consider myself incredibly lucky to have met Caius.

Chapter Nine
Luck Is What You Make It

Luck.

Some people have it, some don't. My luck, left to its own devices, tends to be fairly average. I can't complain about having chronically bad luck, but good luck's never done me any unusual favors either—unless I ask for it.

So, I might have spent a little quality time with my ritual circle last night, and said quality time may or may not have resulted in there being a warrant approval waiting for me Thursday morning when I got to work. It's certainly possible that the judge would've signed off on it without asking the powers that be for a little help, but I wouldn't have held my breath considering the only evidence presented was a moderately sketchy certificate of death, hunches, and a statement from a nurse suspecting foul play.

Precisely why I used a little magic.

We still need to tread cautiously, however. Despite being legit, this warrant is still on shaky legal ground and might not stand up to an aggressive defense lawyer. Perhaps The Goddess helped convince a judge to sign off on a warrant that he might have otherwise had misgivings about. However, I'm not looking to arrest anyone with it, merely find more evidence. A future warrant would come from that evidence, which makes it less likely that a lawyer will think to go all the way back down the warrant chain and challenge the first one. Of course, if they do that and somehow win, the entire thing might fall apart.

Unless I'm lucky.

The nice thing here is that I'm not truly the beneficiary of the spell, the victims are. All I'm personally gaining out of this is the satisfaction of stopping a killer. Assuming, of course, there *is* a killer here, and the situation doesn't merely appear that way. My track record on gut feelings is pretty good, but that's still not proof.

Rick walks in at 7:04 a.m. The frustration etched around his eyes makes it clear he got stuck in traffic.

"Morning." I hold up the warrant. "This might cheer you up."

He folds his arms, unimpressed.

"Wow, must've been a rough ride into work."

"Don't even get me started." He claps his hands in front of his chest, fake-meditating like a Shaolin monk. "So what's the warrant for?"

"Hospital records from Olympia Health Services Hospital. Any files connected to William Johnston. Patients he had contact with who died, disciplinary actions, employee or patient complaints."

Now he looks impressed. "Who'd you have to bribe to get that?"

I shrug. "No one. Guess I got lucky and drew a sympathetic judge."

He points at me. "You drive. Bad things might happen if I get behind the wheel again within the next few hours."

Laughing, I lock my computer and stand. "Sure thing."

Rick turns, heading right back to the door he came in, finger in the air. "There will be coffee!"

***

About twenty minutes and a Starbucks run later, we walk into the administrative office of the hospital.

The first person I approach, a barely-out-of-college blonde woman, has a mild panic attack the instant she sees the badge and warrant, and darts off to get her supervisor. An older woman emerges from the hallway a moment later, with the younger clerk in tow.

"Sorry," says the blonde to us. "I've only been here for a month and I didn't want to make a mistake."

"No problem," says Rick.

"I'm Cassandra Morgan." The other woman, early fifties maybe, shakes our hands with a firm grip and a pleasant nod of greeting. She definitely has a managerial vibe to her. "Kim says you've got a search warrant?"

"That's right." I show her the document and explain what we're looking for.

"Ahh, yes. Very well. I'll help you." She starts walking back down the hall, gesturing for us to follow. "This way, please."

She leads us to her office, comfortably large but modest in decoration. "One moment. I'll need to get someone from legal here."

"Not a problem," says Rick.

Soon, a fortyish man in a grey suit with a short afro joins us, introducing himself as Lionel Barr. Rick, of course, struggles to contain a smile, evidently finding amusement in a lawyer named 'Barr.' The man reviews the warrant and doesn't raise any complaints or objections so Cassandra begins helping us by navigating the computer and pulling up-slash-printing the relevant documents.

William Johnston received two official reprimands related to his being caught in rooms for patients to which he hadn't been assigned. Prior to that, he'd received two verbal and one written warning for the same. One of the written warnings involved Patricia Holcomb; however, it had occurred two months prior to her sudden death.

Rick emits a 'hmm' of suspicion when he

notices that.

None of the other deceased patients mentioned in the warnings/reprimands died under suspicious circumstances, though all of them appear to have been either quite old or in bad shape.

"Rick, look at this." I lean closer to him so he can see the papers with the patient details. "Do you notice any common threads here?"

I watch him compare ethnicities, gender, age, health condition. The gears in his brain practically grind loud enough to make noise. "They're all kinda old, except for those two." He points.

He seems to be fixating on age, so I lean in closer and lower my voice. "Near death is the common thread here, Rick. Including the two younger patients. Metastasized cancer and end-stage ALS. Both dire situations." I frown. "This guy might think he's doing these people a favor by ending their suffering. Or… maybe our suspicions are woefully off base and he's merely looking in on anyone who's knocking on death's door."

Rick gives me his 'and pigs will fly' look.

"Ms. Morgan?" I ask, stepping back over to her desk.

"Mrs." She smiles. "And yes?"

"Of these five patients, did any of them pass away while staying in this hospital?"

She looks at something on her screen. "Reginald Morley did, though he had a rather aggressive form of bone cancer."

"Any irregularities with the death? Was William

Johnston on shift at the time or shortly before?"

"Hmm. No. He wasn't even in that day. Mr. Johnston works the overnight shift on Monday, Wednesday, and Friday, part time. Mr. Morley passed away on a Sunday afternoon. Johnston would've been out the door here at five in the morning the preceding Saturday."

Rick rubs his chin and gives me a dubious glance.

The nurse, Kaitlyn, who first came to us to report the issue, mentioned her fellow nurses all had misgivings about this guy, but the files don't have any records of complaints. When I ask about that, Cassandra and Lionel accompany us over to the HR office.

A somewhat pudgy and *way* too happy/enthusiastic woman named Renee pulls up Johnston's employee file. No complaints listed there either, so either the administration brushed them aside or the nurses had only been commiserating amongst themselves about their feelings. According to this file, Johnston started at Olympia Health Services Hospital five months plus one week ago. His last employer is shown as St. Bartholomew's Hospital… which is about ten miles from here.

Hmm. Either Johnston got tired of dealing with religious staff, this place pays more, or something happened over there.

Rick and I spend another hour or so rooting around the records while Cassandra and Lionel either assist us or observe, but don't find anything more helpful than the record of the reprimands and warnings. After thanking them for their time, we head out.

When we reach our car, Rick glances at me across the roof. "That isn't exactly what I'd call productive."

"Nor was it a complete waste of time." I hold the papers up. "Being caught in the wrong patient rooms multiple times is a red flag."

"Maybe a pink flag."

I raise an eyebrow. "Where are you going with that one?"

"Just that it's not instantly alarming. It's suspicious but not proof. Not fully red."

"Ahh. Shall we try Saint Bart's?"

Rick pulls the door open and gets in. "Might as well."

I hop in.

"But that warrant's no good there."

"Nothing wrong with asking nicely first." I smile.

He chuckles. "That's true. Gonna hide your jewelry?"

"I'm a little annoyed at the suggestion that I have to hide my symbols of belief so as not to offend people who don't hold the same beliefs." I start the engine, stifling a sigh. "No, I'm not directing that at you. I know you're right. Sucks to be in the minority. At least they stopped burning us alive."

He gives me a 'not touching that' look, picks up his now-cold coffee out of the cup holder, and drinks the last third or so he had left in one long gulp.

Right. It's a hospital affiliated with a church, not an actual church. A handful of pentacle amulets won't cause a problem, right?

Chapter Ten
Sick Burn

Upon arriving at St. Bartholomew's Hospital in northwest Olympia, we make our way to the administrative area via a mixture of asking for directions and flashing our badges.

Eventually, we end up in the office of head nurse Josef Koch, a severe man with black hair so short it almost looks like a substance he's smeared on his scalp. In contrast to his narrow face, thin cheeks, and hard eyes, he offers a warm smile and a voice totally unlike what I expect—soft and gentle, with a hint of a German accent.

"Hello, detectives." Josef stands and leans over his desk to shake our hands before gesturing at two facing chairs. "Please, have a seat and tell me what I can do for you."

Rick's still giving me this weird little smile

since no one has yet commented about my jewelry. I haven't even gotten any bizarre looks.

Since he's being quiet, I take point. "We're looking into the background of a nurse who formerly worked at this hospital. Unfortunately, I can't really divulge too much about the case at this time. We were hoping you could share with us anything unusual about a Mr. William Johnston."

Josef's eyebrows inch up; instant name recognition. "Ahh, yes. Him. Yes, Mr. Johnston had some issues. I can't say I personally cared for him much. Other members of the nursing staff routinely complained that he gave off 'bad vibes.' They didn't like the way he looked at them or skulked around. Off the record, I'm glad he's no longer employed here. You won't find much by way of the complaints in the official record. The administration didn't like to call attention to such things. When his behavior became enough of an issue, they asked him to resign."

"Over complaints from other nurses?" I ask. "Did they threaten to all quit if he wasn't fired?"

Josef shakes his head. "No, it didn't get to that point. Something else happened. A patient…" He pauses, looking back and forth between us. "Are you investigating William for murdering patients in his care?"

I sit up a little straighter. "You suspect he'd be capable of that?"

"No, detective. I suspect he *did* that." Josef makes an annoyed face at the door, then lowers his voice. "There was a patient here, Stephen Abbott, a twenty-eight-year-old man brought in with burns over most of his body. He looked fairly... ah, gruesome, but as I remember, the doctors expected he would survive, albeit with significant scarring. The man died suddenly overnight after four days. I'm not privy to the exact cause of death, but William resigned soon after. As I understand, he had been *encouraged* to resign."

"And in your opinion, Mr. Johnston had something to do with the death of Stephen Abbott?" I ask.

Josef nods.

Rick looks up from his notepad after finishing writing a line. "Is there anything more than complaints and rumors that brought you to that opinion?"

"Mr. Johnston had been caught checking on patients outside his assigned rounds numerous times. He also used a forged signature to obtain drugs from the hospital pharmacy on at least one occasion."

I jot down *forged, stole drugs from hosp pharm.* "Do you know what drug was taken?"

He tilts his head back, eyes closed, lost in thought for a few seconds. "Might have been Fentanyl, pentobarbital, or possibly digoxin."

I note them all.

"So the patient, in this case, was neither old nor terminal?" Rick shifts his weight to the side.

"No on both counts. However, Mr. Abbott

would not likely have had a normal life. Facial disfigurement often has an adverse reaction on quality of living. I believe the man also lost most of his fingers."

I cringe, squeezing my hands into fists as if to protect my fingers from an imaginary fire.

"Ouch," mutters Rick. "Poor guy."

"Excuse me for a moment, I need to call back to the station." I stand and move off to the corner of the office to call the captain while Rick keeps talking to Josef. Hope she's not in the middle of something.

"Talk to me, Wims," says Captain Greer.

"I think we're really onto something here, Captain. Rick and I are at St. Bart's hospital where our suspect worked prior to OHSH. There's another patient here who suffered a mysterious death. Also, they have a record of our guy using falsified documents to obtain drugs from the in-house pharmacy. Any chance you could have them amend the warrant to include records about Johnston here, too?"

"Give me the details."

I pass along everything we got from Josef.

"All right. Give me a few minutes."

"Thanks, Cap."

I return to the chair. Rick and Josef chat for a little while about Johnston, mostly gossip from other nurses who said the guy often looked *through* people rather than at them. He didn't talk to anyone unless someone else initiated a conversation—which didn't happen often—or his work required him to speak. Patients occasionally complained about his being aloof or condescending, once even flat out ignoring them as if he'd zoned out.

This guy sounds like he's almost certainly got some mental issues. Well, given he's murdering people—I assume—mental problems tend to go without saying to some degree. Just how much, though, is the bigger question.

Rick glances over. "How'd it go with Greer?"

"Waiting on a callback."

"For?" asks Josef.

"With a little luck, a judge will extend our existing search warrant so we can officially request any records regarding this issue."

Josef nods. "I still can't understand why the administration simply swept this all under the rug."

"Was there a lawsuit from Abbott's family?" asks Rick.

"I'm not sure. Since I don't remember hearing about it, I'm guessing not."

"Did the family—" My phone ringing makes me jump. "Sorry. One sec. Gotta take this." Since it's Greer's ringtone, I'm not inclined to ignore it... but I also don't bother wandering off to the corner again. "Hey, Captain."

"Judge Warnock was in a good mood. You've got authorization to request personnel records for William Johnston as well as the records of any patient deemed to have died unexpectedly while he had access to them."

"Great. Thank you, Captain."

"Don't thank me too much. The judge somehow agreed with your suspicions."

"Just lucky I guess." I make an innocent face at Rick.

"A little too lucky sometimes," says Greer, though a smile is clear in her voice. "I trust you'll call it a day if it looks like it's going nowhere. If you need a hardcopy, text me a fax number."

I look at Josef. "Do you have a fax machine?"

He nods, and gives me the number, which I relay to the captain.

"Couple minutes," says Greer.

"Well?" asks Rick after I swipe the call off.

"We're good to go." I stuff the phone back in its belt holder. "Warrant should be coming over soon."

***

Two hours later, Rick and I are in a different office with the hospital manager, Tobias Weir, two lawyers, and a small cluster of clerks and middle-managers. We look over the files related to Stephen Abbott. His cause of death is listed as respiratory arrest with subsequent cardiovascular collapse as a result of pentobarbital (Nembutal) overdose. His blood tests showed he had been given a dose equivalent to fifteen grams, with death likely occurring within twelve minutes of injection.

Two things are quite obvious to me after looking these documents over. One: Stephen Abbott was murdered. Two: the hospital knew it.

Maybe I should consider 'murdered' as jumping to a conclusion. I suppose a man in a medically-induced coma to spare him the pain of severe burns could have spontaneously awoken, decided to end his own life, and set about raiding the pharmacy for a lethal drug before crawling back into bed and hooking up all the IVs and whatnot, then injecting himself.

Yeah, right.

He was murdered.

"Mr. Wier," I say, glancing over at the manager, a suave late-forties type in a nice suit with perfect brown hair and an intense tanning-bed junkie tone to his skin. He looks more like he should be on the cover of GQ than the manager for a hospital run by a religious organization. Thus far, he's been obligatorily cooperative, offering only a few annoyed glances as any form of protest to our investigation. "From what I'm reading here, I get the feeling that the administration was fully aware that Mr. Abbott's death appeared to be an intentional homicide. Why wasn't this reported to the county medical examiner or the police?"

"We weren't able to conclusively determine who made the dosage error. St. Bartholomew's accepted responsibility for the mistake and settled privately with the family."

Rick fires off a 'you gotta be shittin' me' stare at the guy. "Dosage error? The deceased was comatose in bed at the time of his death. Someone got in there and shot him up with that nebulous stuff."

"Nembutal," I mutter.

Weir hesitates. The argument circling his brain almost leaks out into the room, though I'm not sure if he's more afraid of us going after him (or the hospital in general) or additional lawsuits. "The man you're investigating, William Johnston... we believed he is the one responsible. However, we had no way to prove it. The board decided that it would be in the best interest of the hospital and its patients if Mr. Johnston's employment ended voluntarily."

"So," I say, raising an eyebrow. "You asked him to resign and threatened to report him to the police if he didn't?"

"Finding the evidence to prove who killed someone is our job. That's not the hospital's responsibility," adds Rick, mildly heated. "At least two other people are dead now."

Weir fidgets. "You have to understand, detectives... this wasn't my decision to make. The board considered all angles."

"Especially liability," says Rick. "God. How could you just set a guy like that loose on the city?"

I put a hand on my partner's arm, not intentionally trying to play 'good cop,' but he's getting a little too pissed. "Did the Nembutal originate from St. Bart's pharmacy?"

"That's part of the problem, detective." Weir shakes his head. "We didn't have any Nembutal go missing. Or any other variant of pancuronium bromide. I'm sure if we would've been able to link Mr.

Johnston to an improper requisition for Nembutal which had subsequently been used to end Mr. Abbott's life, we absolutely would have involved the police right away. I believe the board was concerned that a criminal investigation would fail, which may have ultimately led Mr. Johnston to sue the hospital for wrongful termination, claiming we made up the accusation to get rid of him."

Rick massages his sinuses. "I know I'm a cop, but sometimes the law can be a real pain in the ass. When did people stop caring about doing the *right* damn thing and only worried about dollar signs?"

"He's not really looking for an answer," I say in a half-whisper while smiling at the lawyer. "Speaking of answers… can we see his personnel record?"

William Johnston had numerous documented complaints from other nurses. Unlike OHSH, the nurses here apparently had no qualms about airing their concerns to their supervisors. Something tells me Josef has a lot to do with that. The guy struck me as a straight shooter, caring, too. Even if he does look a bit like a young Moff Tarkin. Seriously, I thought he was going to be a total prick at first sight.

Guess looks really are deceiving.

The complaints all sound familiar: he got caught in rooms he shouldn't be in, got caught messing around with patient's medical devices with no good reason. He had also worked the graveyard shift here —oddly appropriate—so would have been in the hospital at the time of Stephen Abbott's death. As a nurse, I imagine he would know that a Nembutal overdose can be detected. Either he trusted himself enough to believe it couldn't be traced back to him, he anticipated that he would be asked to quit rather than arrested if they blamed him for it, or—most scary of all—didn't care.

More and more, I'm starting not to like this case.

I think we're dealing with a true psychopath.

Hope he's not also a clown.

Chapter Eleven
Dead Ends

After finishing up at St. Bart's, we head back to the station by way of a Chinese restaurant.

While munching on my lo mein take out, I decide to throw a wide net. Rick likes my suggestion, so we both comb over city records in search of any similar deaths. Specifically, we're looking for people who died unexpectedly while hospitalized, especially with anomalous circumstances. Given what I've seen so far of hospital administration—at least at those two places—I'm not holding my breath that something like this would've been properly reported to a county coroner.

The afternoon is a miasma of boredom, but we both keep sifting through records despite the world going blurry from staring at a screen so long. Rick's started to get a little silly, talking out loud to the names of patients, 'scolding' them for getting old or dying, or both. He randomly blurts things like, 'Aww, Mrs. Smith, why'd you have to go and turn ninety?' for the better part of two hours. A little after four, I find an entry that catches my attention.

Rather, two linked entries that someone else evidently thought suspicious.

Two men died while patients of an entirely different hospital, Thurston County Ultimacare Pavilion. Both had been in the same wing of the building during their stay—the room numbers are three apart—and died within a month of each other.

Kevin Huang, thirty at the time of death seven months ago, passed away unexpectedly in the evening. The hospital reported his death to the police as suspicious, thinking that a family member may have euthanized him. I pull up the coroner's report. It lists the cause of death as acute hypogly-cemic shock consistent with a massive intravenous dose of insulin. Alas, there's nothing in this report about any other underlying medical condition, so he doesn't fit the profile. Thirty years old and apparently healthy is not the sort of person a 'mercy killer' targets. Then again, they simply might have left it off the paperwork I can get to from here. Otherwise healthy men that age don't wind up in the hospital without *something* being wrong.

The second man, Orson Gunn—wow what a name—was ninety-four at the time of his death, which occurred twenty-five days earlier than Huang. His coroner report blames 'natural causes,' unsurprising for a man his age. However, a Detective Rooney with the northeast precinct homicide division tagged this file, linking it to Huang's record. As best I can tell, the only connection between the two men had been physical proximity at the time of death.

I call over to Northeast, spend the obligatory two minutes making chitchat with the desk sergeant before she transfers me to Rooney, who happens to be there. Wow. Seriously, my luck is holding out. I should probably do another ritual soon to thank the Goddess for being so generous.

"You got Rooney."

"Ack. Is it contagious?" I ask.

He chuckles. "From the sound of your voice, possibly."

"Sorry to rain on your parade there, but I'm engaged."

"Darn. So, who do I have the pleasure of getting shot down by?"

"Detective Wimsey, Homicide at Central. Got a couple questions about a case you worked on a little over a year ago."

A chair creak comes over the line. Guess their furniture is as old as ours. "Sure. Shoot."

I explain what's going on, then bring up the Huang death. "You cross-linked the record to another patient who also died there."

"Yeah, the older-than-dirt guy. Had a weird name. Ormond or something."

"Orson."

"Right. That."

"Why'd you link the file? There's nothing terribly surprising about a ninety-four-year-old with a six-page list of medical conditions passing away in his sleep." Seriously, that poor man had a whole lot of problems. A good third of them, I'd never even heard of and still probably couldn't pronounce right under pressure.

"A night nurse at the place suggested I look into his death as well. Didn't have any proof beyond a hunch, and you gotta know how accurate hunches can be. Figure a nurse getting a hunch about a patient dying can't be any less accurate than ones we get about a suspect. So, I did a little poking around. Guy in the morgue told me Orson suffered a severe hemorrhage. That's internal bleeding."

"Yeah, I know." Sigh.

"So, Orson bleeds to death internally. The morgue guy, Phil I think his name was, gave me the feeling he doubted the old dude would spring such a leak out of the blue, despite all he had going wrong. But… you know…"

"Who'd think someone that old and sick passing away in their sleep was unusual at all," I say.

"Yeah. Exactly."

I stare at the ceiling and hold back a frustrated groan. "Do you think the administration knew something and wanted to hide it or do you think they just cut corners and assumed the hemorrhage was due to his advanced age?"

"Probably had to do with liability," says

Rooney. "You know, didn't want anyone to sue them."

"Yes, Detective Rooney, I know what liability means."

Rick twists around in his chair to glance at me. His expression says 'oh, one of those.'

I nod at him, rolling my eyes. "What did you find out about Huang?"

"Sec, let me check my notes." Key clicking serenades me for a minute or two. "Okay, here we are… Kevin Huang. Guy was only thirty. Poor bastard. So, the hospital suspected one of his family members euthanized him; meaning, you know, killed him for like mercy."

By the grace of the Goddess, I don't growl into the phone. "Yes, I do understand what euthanasia is. I'm aware that Mr. Huang experienced a massive overdose of insulin that brought on a state of extreme hypoglycemic shock which further led to acute cerebral hypoxia, irreversible brain damage, multiple organ shutdown, and death."

Hey, I'm reading the file, but I *sound* like a doctor. And yeah, I do mostly understand all of that.

Rooney 'umms.'

Rick gives me a thumbs-up.

My little 'f-you' smile at the phone makes him snicker. I continue: "The report doesn't tell me why Huang wound up in the hospital in the first place or why his family would've wanted to euthanize him. Speaking of which, what did you determine?"

"Umm," says Rooney, again. "He had something they called locked-in syndrome. No idea how he got it, but they described it as a really horrible way to go."

I remember hearing about that condition on the news, at least enough to correct him. "I didn't think locked-in syndrome was inherently fatal... just awful."

"Well, yeah. You know what I mean. Guy's like totally paralyzed. Can't move, can't talk, nothin'. Sheesh. He probably *wanted* to die. Anyway, the dude came home from work early and caught a burglar in his house who, in the resulting altercation, stabbed Mr. Huang in the head. He'd been completely paralyzed, unable to communicate with anyone for about two years before he died. I spoke to his younger sister, parents, grandparents... none of them checked out as possible killers. The sister could barely speak she cried so much over his death. Grandparents were pretty upset, too. I can see how the hospital staff might have thought the parents might've been involved. As far as I'm concerned, they didn't do it, but I do think they believed their son was better off dead than living on in that state."

I nod while writing notes. "Did you have any suspects at the time? You know, people you think might have done it."

Rick chuckles.

So does, Rooney. At least the guy has a sense of humor. "Heh. Nice one. Ehh, was batting around a theory of hospital error. Was thinking someone might've effed up and given the guy insulin by accident instead of whatever medicine they should've given him. Maybe threw suspicion on the family to cover it."

"Detective," I say. "Given that the hospital itself reported the death to the police as suspicious, wouldn't that tend to imply they *weren't* trying to cover things up?"

"One would think," says Rooney with a note of triumph. "But reporting the death would be the perfect way to make it look like it *wasn't* a hospital error. For exactly the reason you're thinking."

Oh, boy… I lean back and sigh.

"But… I couldn't track down where the dose came from. All the nurses and doctors checked out. The time of Huang's death put the injection well after visiting hours. The hospital pharmacy reported no unexplained loss of insulin. They did have a shortage of two other drugs, but the pharmacist hadn't been convinced at the time it wasn't a bookkeeping error. Umm…" A few more key clicks rattle my eardrum. "Heparin and Nembutal."

"Nembutal?"

"That's what I said. Heparin and Nembutal."

Rick looks at me like a hunting dog eyeing a duck.

"One of my victims was killed with Nembutal, but the hospital where it happened wasn't missing any of that. Huang died six months ago, right? My suspect stopped working at St. Bart's five months ago. He could've stolen the Nembutal from Thurston County Ultimacare Pavilion."

"We started calling it teacup for short. T-C-U-P," says Rooney.

"Right... Do you remember a nurse named William Johnston?"

"The name doesn't ring a bell... and I don't see it in my notes."

"Damn. So you think Huang was killed intentionally or died due to a gross error?"

"Couldn't tell."

I smile. "What's your gut say?"

He laughs. "Time for dinner. But, about that case? I kinda suspected the father found a nurse willing to put Kevin out of his misery and paid them off."

"Did you find any suspicious financial activity on the father's accounts?"

"Nope. But that doesn't prove he didn't have some cash stuffed in his mattress. Huang's currently in my cold case fridge. You thinking your body is connected to my body?"

In your dreams, bud. It takes a lot of self-control not to make a wise-ass comment. "If I can place Johnston at TCUP, then yes. Speaking of which, I'm going to piss off my partner and insist on running over there before our shift ends."

"Good luck. Let me know if you find anything."

"Thanks." I hang up the desk phone and bury my face in my hands. "Ugh. Total mansplainer."

Rick chuckles while standing and grabbing his coat. "I wish I could've seen his face when you hit him over the head with that jargon bomb."

I snicker. "It wasn't a jargon bomb... technically. I knew what I said."

"You and them fancy books." He winks.

I stick my tongue out at him.

Real mature, right?

"I take it we're hitting the bricks," says Rick.

"Hitting them hard. Let's go."

Chapter Twelve
Cold Tea

The Thurston County Ultimacare Pavilion logo actually is a teacup.

Guess Rooney's not so original after all.

Everything here is either white or silver-chrome. Here and there, they have these random slabs of brickwork or stone in the walls that seem out of place, like artifacts from antiquity. Either that or the hipster fairy went traipsing about with her wand, firing bolts of 'trendy retro' at the décor. This whole hospital radiates a 'we probably don't take your peasant insurance' vibe. Or, maybe the spaceship-like ultramodern architecture is throwing me off.

It only takes us five minutes to end up in the office of their VP of legal, Vivian Prescott. Two degrees, one law and one business, hang prominently on the wall behind her desk. She looks mid-thirties with black hair in a strange up-do that I can't quite tell if it's futuristic or retro, ghostly pale face, and all the emotional range of a Roomba.

Between this woman and the building's design, it's as if I've walked into a cyberpunk dystopia. I'm half tempted to ask her if she's a human.

"Detectives?" asks Vivian. "What is it I can help you with?"

"We're following up on a case regarding the deaths of two patients under suspicious circumstances."

Vivian nods once, her motion curt and precise. Almost choreographed... or the result of an android servo. Of course, there aren't any such things as androids. "I'm afraid I'm not at liberty to discuss the specifics of patient records in the absence of a search warrant. Do you have one?"

"We do, but it hasn't been updated to include this hospital or these patients yet. This is new information we've only recently become aware of."

"I see. Well, I would be happy to help you as soon as the paperwork is in order."

Damn. She's technically right, but it's annoying. "Okay. We can come back Monday. Not like there's a chance another patient could be killed or anything bad like that."

Vivian's demeanor of total detached calm doesn't flinch in the slightest. "Very well. Have a nice day, detectives."

I start to turn away, but stop myself. "One question. Can you at least confirm the employment of a nurse named William Johnston?"

"Just asking if he worked here or not," says Rick. "Any HR department will answer yes or no to that over the phone."

Vivian again offers the same precise nod, then presses a finger to her desktop. A thin computer screen rises up from what formerly appeared to be solid glass. For a second, I really do think I've gone forward in time… at least until I see the Apple logo. She smoothly lowers herself to sit at the chair and types away on a capacitance keyboard—like an iPhone screen—embedded in the desktop. Her pale fingers flash cobalt blue in the light glowing from under the glass.

"No one by that name has worked here as a nurse or in any other capacity."

Drat. Drat, times two. I glare down at the floor, trying to come up with a way to get this woman to talk to us. A spot of black catches my eye, perched on the rim of a thin silver wastebasket beside the desk. Hair. Wow, did this woman do her own hair while in the office? That looks like a brush clump. If she managed to get her hair into that shape herself, that's almost more impressive than earning dual degrees in her mid-thirties. Still, the tuft on the wastebasket is the same shade of black and apparently hung on the rim due to an inaccurate throw.

I pull out my phone. "One moment, just referring to some notes." Instead of reading, I send Rick a text: distract her a sec plz. Then, I look up. "Can you comment on the disappearance of Nembutal from the pharmacy?"

Rick twitches and checks his phone.

"I'm afraid I'd need to have a warrant. For legal reasons, of course."

"Right," I mutter.

"Well, I guess we're about done here, then." Rick stands up fast and hip-bumps the desk hard enough to knock over a small vase, which sends water splashing out. "Gah!"

Vivian's eyes flare wide in alarm. She ducks to open a lower drawer on the right. The instant she's no longer looking at me, I swipe the hair clump and stuff it in my jacket pocket. Vivian pops back up with a bottle of pre-moistened cleaning wipes.

"Those aren't going to help," says Rick. "Need a sponge or paper towels. Really sorry about that. Big feet. Sometimes I trip over them." He points to the right. "That a bathroom?"

"Yes," says Vivian, still sounding neutral. She pulls a wipe from the can and pushes it into the water flow.

Rick runs to get paper towels. Fortunately, the entire desktop—except for where the screen popped up—appears to be a solid sheet of glass, so the water doesn't get into anything electronic. My partner returns with a handful of towels and helps mop up. He's good at playing the uncoordinated oaf.

Once the vase is again standing and refilled—it is a fairly small one, glass with glass beads—we let ourselves out. When we reach the atrium, well out of earshot of the office, Rick gives me the inquisitive glance.

"Hair."

"What did it do this time?"

I chuckle. "Not mine. No, I nabbed some of hers from the wastebasket."

"Ahh. Planning to boost the chances of a search warrant?"

"Something like that." I pat the pocket. The hair, of course, was about to be ingredient #1 in my next ritual. "Goddess willing, Vivian might be more cooperative by Monday."

He shakes his head, almost smiling. "It's only my not-quite belief that's keeping me from being party to breaking the law."

I stop, glancing over at him with an overacted innocent face. "Which statute prohibits the use of magical assistance in questioning a non-cooperating potential witness?"

"Ehh… let me get back to you on that one."

"I didn't think it bothered you." I hit the button for the elevator down to the parking area.

He leans on the wall. "It doesn't. Not when you do it. What unsettles me is the idea if that stuff works for you, what could someone else without your deep sense of karmic balance do with it?"

I wag my eyebrows. "You really don't want to know."

The elevator opens with a *ding*.

Rick exhales, lips flapping. "Right. Forget I asked."

Chapter Thirteen
No More Clowning Around

Caius has a lovely dinner of lobster ravioli waiting for me when I get home.

He thinks he 'cheated' by using premade pasta sheets, even if he did stuff the ravioli himself with a filling he'd made by hand. As busy as he can be with his music business, whenever he decides to take a day off—or just happens to have time—he cooks. It's like zen for him.

After we eat, there's serious cuddle time in the living room while he puts on the new *Blade Runner* movie. That almost makes me laugh out loud given that I felt like I'd been *in* the first movie this afternoon. He tends to spend most of the time we spend watching movies commenting on the score more than the acting, cinematography, or plot. Considering his passion is music, I totally understand that.

I'm so comfortable I almost don't want to move. We could sleep right here on this giant black sectional and it would be paradise. Alas, it's next to impossible for me to be content while a killer is out there somewhere. Amendment: a killer I know of and am pursuing. There's technically *always* a killer out there somewhere.

"Need to pester The Goddess again," I say in a half whisper.

Caius brushes his hand at my hair and kisses me lightly on the temple. "Another bad case?"

"I work homicide investigations. They're all bad. Maybe I'm simply being impatient here, but better we stop this guy fast. The longer it takes, the more people he can hurt."

"Understood. Need help?"

"If you want. Not doing a big spell, just a little nudge."

He leans close, seemingly drinking in my scent before kissing my neck. The heat of his lips on my skin shoots tiny lightning bolts down my body straight into my toes. He slips a hand under my oversized T-shirt, sliding it over my hip to my side. Oh, if he keeps that up, I'm going to entirely forget about doing any magic tonight. It's so tempting to wriggle out of the shirt and entwine my body with his. As he so often does at home, he's wearing only a pair of loose black silk pants that kind of make him look like a skinny samurai. We hold and caress each other for a little while longer before I emit a soft, contented moan and twist to face him, our noses nearly touching.

"It won't take long. You're trying to start a much more involved—and fun—spell than the one I need to do. We can get back to *this* spell in a little while."

"I shall be as a lover upon the shore longing for the second half of their soul to return from afar."

A grin spreads across my face. "I'm only going to the yard, not off to war."

"The separation will be no less painful," he says, also smiling.

I poke him in the side, making him laugh, then slip away to my little indoor garden. There, I gather a few passion flower petals. The basis for this little spell is going to be friendship. Hopefully, it will nudge Veronica into being more cooperative. Next, I pluck some raspberry leaf to add a layer of protection for both of us, then cloves for luck. My plan is to extend the luck to her as well, causing the spell to provide her as much or more benefit than it manipulates her. Last, I add several camellia sasanqua leaves, an herb used to express gratitude, which I am directing toward the Goddess for her blessing of luck.

At my work table, I perch on the stool, one foot up under my rear end, and assemble two sachets. The one I'll burn as an offering to The Goddess gets the bulk of the camellia. The other will be hanging around my neck when next I visit Vivian. Into that one, I stuff a pinch of hair I took from her wastebasket. Finally, I take a slip of paper and write a letter as if to Vivian herself, asking her to trust me with whatever she knows about the case and to set aside her fears of policy, lawsuits, or whatever personal sense of victory she may derive from being able to ignore the police. I write that my intention is to seek justice for the victims of a man I believe to be a killer, and to call down the eyes of The Goddess upon myself and Vivian to tilt luck in our favor for a short while.

That done, I fold the paper neatly into a square and seal it with wax.

It's a little chilly outside to wear nothing more than a big T-shirt, but I don't plan to be out there that long and the exhilaration of the cold is as much an embrace from the spirits of nature as anything can be. As a younger woman, Abigail once visited some witches near the Ural Mountains. They'd often dance sky clad in the woods around a bonfire with a foot of snow on the ground. The mere thought of it makes me shiver, but I guess if you grow up in that climate…

I arrange the candles, herbs, and incense on our concrete pentacle in the yard, then open the circle, inviting The Goddess, Cernunnos, as well as the five elements into my circle. I also request the attention of Ma'at, goddess of truth, justice, and order, to oversee this incantation. If my search for this man I believe to be a killer is worthy, may she allow the spell to function.

Once I've opened the circle and feel the

presence of spiritual eyes upon me, I place the offering sachet in a metal bowl at the center of the pentacle, then rest the other pouch beside it. I sprinkle incense flakes into the bowl, add the remainder of the hair, and dust it with about a teaspoonful of dried allspice. Since I'm not looking to keep this woman as a long term friend, I skip the orange candle.

"Wall of fear by wayside crumble,
"Down the path to truth you tumble.
"Lady Prescott with hair of black,
"Receive the trust you sorely lack.

I light the paper with a candle and drop it into the bowl, igniting the contents.

"Fire take my offering high,
"My gratitude to Goddess flies.
"Three times 'round the candles see,
"My words take form, so mote it be."

I kneel there in meditative silence watching the flames within the bowl consume the incense, the paper, and the sachet of camellia. As the little cloth bag burns, I concentrate on how grateful I am that the Goddess so often grants me her blessings. Once the bowl holds only ash, I work the circle widdershins, thanking the Goddess, Cernunnos, the five elements, and Ma'at for their attention.

The circle closed, I clean up the area, gather the remaining sachet, and hurry back inside where it's warm.

There's a Caius waiting for me in the bedroom… and I don't want to delay any longer.

***

Monday morning, I drag myself into the station while sipping a mocha latte with two extra espresso shots—my second cup of coffee so far.

The first one (basic black) didn't last the six minutes it took me to drive from Starbucks to here. Maybe Caius and I stayed up a little too late last night. Admittedly, I'd been slightly uneasy about his idea to try the silk rope and blindfold... but wow. And there's not anyone else on this Earth I'd have trusted. I still don't particularly enjoy being helpless, but with him...

Anyway.

I flop down in my seat and peer at the sachet hanging around my neck atop my array of pentacles and moon amulets. It still feels unusual *not* to get dirty looks from Linda. Detective Gonzalez is our squad's resident Christian. I think she finally accepted that I'm not hostile to her beliefs. I respect them, just don't share them. Wouldn't exactly call us super best buds or anything, but we've gotten closer to the point of being normal co-workers at least.

Rick looks up from his desk as I fall into my chair. "Rough night? You look pale. Well, paler than usual, and that's saying something."

I chuckle. "No, far from rough. Quite tender actually. Just stayed up too late. Weekends aren't long enough."

"Ahh. Nice. So, shall I assume we'll be going to speak to Vivian again?"

"That's the plan. Did the warrant get upgraded yet?"

"Not that I've seen."

Whap.

Something lands on my desk. It's a box of donuts. Normally, I'd probably have half jumped out of my chair at a sudden noise like that so close… but I'm tired, so I merely look up at Ed Parrish. His expression is part way between ready to pass out and wanting to kiss me.

"You do realize that I couldn't possibly eat an entire dozen donuts myself. And why are you looking at me that way?"

"I'll help," says Rick. "And I'm with her, Ed. What gives?"

Detectives Gonzalez, Washington, Quarrel… and even Captain Greer (plus two random patrol officers nearby) all perk up like prairie dogs at the mention of the d-word.

Ed bows at me like an ancient villager at a temple.

"Hey, stop that. I'm not an object of worship." I poke him in the side.

"You are for the moment." He grins. "Holy shit I can't believe we got the bastard."

"Got who? Wait—The clown guy?" I ask.

Everyone—except Ed—cringes.

"Damn straight. So we set up a stakeout on Michael Alvarez, like you suggested. Guy had a big ass white van in his driveway. Small house, so I guess he keeps all his performing gear in the van to save space. Or maybe it's just easier not to constantly unload it. Anyway, like 1:30 in the morning on Saturday, Quarrel wakes me up because there's a guy breaking into the van. We got him on video planting a bomb inside one of the clown's magic props, intending it to go off right in the middle of his show. EOD guys said it would've been messy. Lots of nails and screws."

I shudder. "Holy shit, that would've hit the children... please tell me you got the bastard."

"We did." Ed nods.

"So what was the guy's deal?" asks Rick. "Did a clown scare him when he was little or something?"

"Don't think so. The guy is a few sandwiches short of a picnic. Thinks that clowns are really aliens from some other planet here to abduct people, and he took it upon himself to protect humanity. I honestly don't think he understands it's all makeup and fake noses. He believes they really look like that."

Rick and I whistle at the same time.

"Completely random," says Detective Quarrel, sidling up alongside Ed. "This guy was randomly targeting anyone who performed as a clown. Sometimes, he'd see one and ignore them. Others, he'd get convinced he'd found an alien spy. He even vandalized several McDonald's mascots, thinking the aliens could watch people through them."

"They're gonna fit him for a white coat,"

mutters Rick, eyeing the donut box.

I flip the lid open and help myself to a glazed, then wave it around in a 'have at it' gesture. "You think he's legit or faking being nuts?"

"Leaning toward actual crazy." Ed swipes a Boston Crème. "But, he's got a date with a psychiatrist today for an evaluation. If he's good enough to fake out an actual doctor, he can sit in a mental hospital instead of prison. Either way, he's off the street."

Quarrel picks up a cruller. "Never did understand why so many people have a hatred of clowns. They never bothered me... until this case."

Captain Greer walks over to claim an apple-filled donut. I chat with her for a bit about the warrant and our case. She hasn't heard back yet from the courthouse, which isn't terribly surprising given it's Monday. Judges move pretty fast when it's an emergency like a missing endangered child and we need to start kicking doors down, but something like this case doesn't get fast-tracked.

Quarrel salutes me with his half-donut. "We're gonna throw a damn party for this one being over."

"Donuts and coffee," says Rick. "I say it's a party already."

Chapter Fourteen
Warm Tea

Vivian Prescott still looks like an android from a science fiction movie when we walk in.

However, as soon as I'm within a few feet of her, reaching out to shake her hand, something amazing happens—she smiles.

"Good morning, detectives," says Vivian. "Back so soon?"

"Just following up. Is there any information you can maybe share with us about the deaths of Kevin Huang and Orson Gunn?"

"Hmm." Vivian regards me with a measuring stare, tapping her foot. "I suppose it wouldn't hurt. We, that is the hospital administration, suspected that something unusual occurred in Mr. Huang's death. That's why we referred it to the police." She moves the vase Rick knocked over last time to a shelf behind her, then sits and activates her high tech retractable monitor. "Another detective looked into the case, but they never issued charges against anyone."

Rick and I sit in the same chairs, watching her type.

She confirms the information I already have, that Mr. Huang died of an insulin overdose and the hospital suspected someone wanted to euthanize him despite the family never having expressed any desire to 'pull the plug' on him before that.

"Regarding Mr. Gunn, our internal autopsy concluded that the cause of death was cerebral hemorrhage triggered by an improperly high dose of heparin. Mr. Gunn *was* being given heparin therapeutically to combat thrombosis... however, the amount in his system at the time of death well exceeded normal levels."

I nod, adding that to my notes. "Is it possible for someone to intentionally administer such a dose with intent to cause death?"

"I'm not a doctor, Detective Wimsey, so my opinion here isn't too helpful. But, considering heparin is a blood thinner that can contribute to internal bleeding, it stands to reason that an intentional overdose might be construed as an attempt to kill."

"That's a new one," mutters Rick. "None of the other would-be victims had been exposed to that particular drug."

"Maybe because Gunn was already taking it," I

say. "And the killer thought an overdose might escape detection or be attributed to error rather than malice?"

"Are you suggesting these patients were killed by an employee?" asks Vivian. "We had assumed... well, we didn't know what happened, to be honest."

I nod. "An employee is our suspicion; however, the man we're investigating doesn't work here. At least, the last time we asked about him, you said he didn't."

"Remind me of his name?"

"William Johnston." I say.

She taps a few glowing keys on the glass desktop. "I'm afraid that's correct. That name doesn't exist in our system."

"Are there any nurses, doctors, orderlies, or anyone else on staff who might have access to patients that have received disciplinary reports or complaints for unusual behavior? Specifically things like going into patient rooms where they haven't been assigned to, odd requests for medicine —like heparin. Olympia Health Services' pharmacy came up short on heparin." I flip back over my notes and find where I wrote that. "Ms. Prescott, has your hospital misplaced any Nembutal by chance?"

She gives me the android stare again, hard enough to see the influence of the sachet around my neck battling her instinct to protect her employer from liability at all costs. I try to give her a little bump with a friendly smile.

Vivian opens another window on her computer,

clicks through a few pages, then sighs. "There are some reports of that, yes. Nembutal, insulin, and digoxin have gone missing."

"Gone missing?" asks Rick. "Did someone break in after it closed?"

"This is a hospital, detective. The pharmacy is available 24/7, though at night there is often only one or two pharmacists staffing it. We take security seriously, especially considering the monetary value of some of the items stored there."

I shift my jaw side to side in thought. "If someone faked forms to request drugs, that wouldn't be reported as theft or 'missing' supplies. Is it more likely that someone paid the pharmacist to look the other way or somehow got past them without being noticed?"

Vivian offers a genuine shrug. "I couldn't even begin to speculate. Though I would hope our pharmacists are not susceptible to bribery. As to your other question... there are a handful of complaints in the system regarding some nurses. Mostly for being short with patients, which often translates to not giving them enough painkillers or insisting on bath time. One has a warning for showing up late too often, and another attempted to forge doctor's requests for morphine, we presume to sell on the street. That woman no longer works here."

"Scamming meds from the pharmacy fits the profile, but not for a drug like morphine. All the ones our guy is taking don't have much resell appeal." I tap my pen on the pad. "Would you mind if we talked to some of the nursing staff?"

"That's fine." Vivian smiles again… It looks so weird on her. "Is there anything else I can help you with?"

"Nothing I can think of right now, but if something comes up, we'll be back."

She nods. "All right. Have a wonderful day."

"You too." I smile and stand.

When Rick gets up, Vivian braces for calamity —but my partner is the perfect picture of grace.

We spend the next three hours walking the halls and chatting up nurses. No one mentions anything suspicious, though one nurse, a late-twenties woman with model looks and dark skin, seems uncomfortable the entire time we're speaking to her. Usually, when someone seems like they can't wait to get away from us, it means they're guilty as hell. However, in this woman's case, I've got the feeling she wants to say something she's afraid to mention where it can be overheard.

So, I hand her a card. "Thanks. If you remember anything, feel free to call us whenever."

"Okay," says the nurse, Tatianna. She studies the card for a few seconds before tucking it into her smock. "I, umm, need to go. On a schedule here." She taps a tray of meds.

"By all means," says Rick. "People need their pills."

She hurries off.

Rick glances at me. "She's gonna call."

"Think so?"

"She's got something she really wants to say, but… not here."

I close my pad and tuck it in my pocket. "Yeah. I got the same vibe off her."

"More magic?"

"Nah. Just a gut feeling."

He chuckles. "Ready for lunch?"

"More than." I start for the elevator at a brisk walk. Too much time inside a hospital is not good for anyone.

Chapter Fifteen
The Pharmacist

Since the drugs went missing from the Thurston County Ultimacare Pavilion pharmacy during the late shift, we decide to drop by the residence of the pharmacist who filed the report. Thanks to the search warrant, we have all the names, addresses and numbers we need.

Trevor Lauten lives in an apartment complex in the northwest part of Olympia. He's probably not doing too bad for himself, at least it's highly doubtful that he'd risk losing his job, his license, and facing prosecution for illegally re-selling medication out of the pharmacy.

He appears quite bleary when he answers the door. The man's tall, lanky, with short-cropped hair that isn't sure if it wants to be light brown or blonde. Based on the one-eye-closed face, plus bathrobe and boxers, I'm sure we woke him up.

"Sorry for dragging you out of bed," I say, holding up my badge. "I'm Detective Wimsey and this is my partner, Detective Santiago."

"Okay..."

"We understand you had some items go missing from the pharmacy. We were hoping you could explain how that happened."

Rick gives him the hard stare. "The hospital assured us that security is rather good."

Trevor rubs his face. "Ugh. Hang on a sec. Not all the way awake yet. Might as well come in." He offers us coffee on the way to his kitchen, where he proceeds to make a pot. "I usually wake up in like an hour anyway, so no big deal."

"Thanks, we're good on coffee." I smile.

"I think the drugs went missing one night when I had a particularly bothersome case of the runs." He hits the button on the coffee maker, then turns to face us, leaning against the counter. "Sorry if that's gross, but there it is. As you can probably imagine given the shift I work, I'm alone. Whenever I need to go to the bathroom, I have to close up and lock the dispensary window. If the drugs went missing during my shift, it would've had to be then. I didn't catch the theft for several days until receiving a valid request for heparin. I noticed the serial number on the bottle didn't match the one I should have been dispensing, so that made me count. One bottle was missing. So, I conducted a full inventory and discovered other losses."

"That had to be tedious," says Rick, softening up some. It is hard not to be won over by the young pharmacist's candor.

"Things are usually pretty quiet at night, so I have time. When someone's going to help themselves to meds, it's usually things they can either use to get high or resell on the streets. The insulin I can understand to a point. Stuff's getting crazy expensive these days."

"What's digoxin?" I ask.

"It's a heart medication used mostly to treat atrial fibrillation or flutter and formerly heart failure. They don't use it as the first choice in cases of full-blown heart failure anymore, since it's been shown to actually increase risk of death."

"Could digoxin be used intentionally to cause death?" asks Rick.

Trevor nods. "Oh, definitely. It has a narrow therapeutic index. The difference between a safe dose and a lethal one isn't much. It can easily cause cardiac arrest."

Rick and I exchange an 'oh shit' glance.

"Do you have any suspicions as to who might be responsible for the theft?" I ask. "Even if it's an out of the blue guess."

"I don't. Hospital security tried to check the video, but whoever did it blacked out the cameras with a view of the pharmacy days before I got the runs."

Rick tilts his head. "And no one noticed this for several days?"

"Those cams aren't live monitored. No one ever looks at the feeds unless they're reviewing them for a specific reason." Trevor pulls the carafe from the coffee maker and pours himself a cup. "You guys sure you don't want some?"

"Nah." I smile. "You look like you need the whole pot. Exactly how I felt this morning."

He chuckles. "This *is* my morning."

"Trevor?" asks Rick. "Would you say your episode of the runs was abnormal?"

"Well, considering I don't habitually go to the toilet four times an hour, yes."

"Heh. No, I mean that in the sense of did you eat something suspect or feel ill other than needing to run to the can every ten minutes? Were you sick enough to expect to have the runs or did they come out of nowhere. I'm wondering if someone slipped you a laxative in order to get you away from your work area."

Trevor's face loses a little color; he freezes with the coffee mug at his lip. "It did seem to come rather out of the blue before I ate lunch that night." He stares down at his drink. "Coffee. Someone might've shot something into my coffee cup. It would've been right there on the desk by the dispensary window. It's possible someone could've approached when I went into the back to fill an order. But... the person with the order would've seen them tamper with my coffee. That means it would've had to have been whoever requested a medication." He taps a finger on his cup. "I'll check over my records tonight and send you a list of everyone who requested medication that night."

I hand him a card. "Great. That would be a huge help."

"Least I can do if what you're implying is really going on." He swallows. "I hope you find them."

"Thanks." Rick shakes his hand.

I do as well. "We really appreciate your help."

Trevor walks us out, yawns, and closes the door behind us.

"Nice to see at least one person not terrified of 'the administration.'" Rick smiles.

"Yeah. No kidding." I jog down the stairs to the parking lot.

Isabelle calls me when I'm halfway to the car, freaking out because the birthday party clown canceled at the last minute. "Holy crap! How did you know he was gonna flake, Mads?"

"Just a guess." I lean on the car door. "And he didn't really flake out. I can't say too much because it's an active investigation, but the poor guy was targeted by a suspect some of my associates have been chasing for weeks. It's not his fault."

"Shit. Is he okay?" asks Isabelle.

Rick gives me a 'what's up?' stare.

I mouth 'Isabelle,' then say, "Physically fine. Probably a little rattled though. Like if a speeding car slams into the wall of a building six feet away from you. Near miss kinda thing."

"Oh, wow. Poor guy. So, anyway, when the clown canceled, we wound up going to this place with like ball pits and games and a dude dressed up like a giant rat. I have *such* a damn headache… but the kids loved it."

"Nice. Hey, would you mind if I called you back a little later?"

"Oops, you're at work. Sure. No problem. Talk later, bye!"

She hangs up before I can say a word.

Rick laughs, no doubt overhearing some of our conversation, and hops in the car.

I sigh and put my phone back in its holder and get in. Truth is, I sometimes wish I had Isabelle's "problems." That is, until I remember I'm pretty good at what I do. And what I do is find killers.

Or try like hell to.

Chapter Sixteen
Under The Rug

The Law of Threefold Return states that whatever energy we send out into the universe comes back to us three times as strong.

This is generally why I'm so hesitant to use magic for anything other than protection or insight. Doing bad things to people via paranormal means almost always ends up biting a witch in the ass. Some who are truly into black magic have ways to divert the blowback onto other people, but that only delays the inevitable—and makes it all that much worse when the giant karmic turd finally comes crashing down on their head.

So, when my desk phone rings one minute before I'm about to go home Monday night, I take my threefold return in stride. I've been asking for luck lately, so a bit of bad luck is to be expected.

Also, it's not like my job is meaningless office crap. Staying late can wind up protecting innocent people.

Again, if I couldn't stand working overtime, I never would've applied to be a detective in the first place.

"Wimsey," I say by way of answering.

"Pardon?" asks a young woman.

"This is Detective Madeline Wimsey."

"Oh. Sorry. We spoke earlier at the hospital. I'm Tatianna Marcus, a nurse?"

I grin and wave at Rick, who's starting to get up to leave. "Yes. I remember you. Thanks for calling. What can I do for you?"

"I couldn't talk at the hospital. Can we meet somewhere?"

"How about the Starbucks across from Sylvester Park?"

"That's perfect. I'll go there right now," says Tatianna.

"Great. See you in a few minutes." I hang up, then look at Rick. "Nurse with information."

He continues putting on his jacket. "Sounds good."

***

The woman's the kind of skinny that Barbie dreams about being.

Without her nurse's scrubs on, she looks like a high-end fashion model. I'm not used to women being that much taller than me. Not that I'm tall or anything, but this girl is a true gazelle. Or giraffe, wait, no, her neck isn't too long. Bleh. Whatever.

She's standing near one of the tables in the back, clutching a cup. As soon as we walk in, she fidgets as if second-guessing her decision to talk to us. Fortunately, she doesn't run. Not sure I could catch a girl ten years younger than me with legs that long.

"Might as well make a meal out of it. You want anything, Wims?" asks Rick.

"No thanks."

He heads over to the register while I join Tatianna at her table. Once I'm there, she sits, as do I.

"I'm sorry I didn't say anything earlier, but they'd fire me as soon as anything for talking to the police. If we say something that could put the hospital in a bad light, they'd call it a breach of patient confidentiality even if it has nothing to do with patients."

I nod. "I'm getting that feeling. It's all right. We'll do as much as we can to keep your name out of things. Depending on what you tell me, you may or may not be called on to testify if a case ever goes to trial. However, if that happens, and they fire you, sue the shit out of them."

She laughs.

"What is it you needed to tell us?" I ask. Might as well get to the point.

"Should I wait for your partner?"

I glance over at Rick, who's staring up at the menu board. "Might as well. He shouldn't take long."

My partner gets an iced tea and a sandwich for dinner, then joins us at the table. "Hope you don't mind if I munch on this while we talk."

Tatianna shrugs at him. "Doesn't bother me. I know how it is. Same for me some nights with the crazy hours. Gotta eat when you can. So, you guys think some patients were killed, right?"

I nod. "It's looking that way."

"Well, there's another nurse at Teacup who really gives me the creeps. Dude tries to be friendly and stuff, but it's like he has no idea how to be around people. Almost like a space alien trying to fake being a human. I'm glad he's only on shift for the weekends. Normally, I don't have to deal with him unless I'm grabbin' overtime or covering for Nellie, this other nurse. Anyway, this dude is like seriously freaky. Gave me the creeps first time I laid eyes on him. And, a couple months ago, I was working a Saturday night and saw him slip a medication bottle into his pocket on the way out of a patient's room, but I wasn't close enough to tell exactly what drug."

Out come the notepads.

"Let's start with this guy's name."

"Gerald. Gerald umm, Peters."

Rick glances at me. "What are the odds we're dealing with a tag team?"

"Fair to reasonable." I jot down the name.

"Also, I've heard people talking. The hospital's been coming up short on several drugs like heparin, digoxin, insulin, and epinephrine that aren't valuable on the street. But, the administration is sweeping it all under the rug for some reason. I saw Gerald walk out of the room of a patient who died later that night, but the poor guy was extremely old... so I guess it could be a coincidence."

"Orson?" I ask.

"Yeah. That's him. He was pretty sweet for such an old guy. Sometimes the real old ones give me a bad attitude for being, you know, dark-skinned. Talk to me like I'm some kind of servant. But Orson kept telling me how he'd take me off on a grand trip around the world as soon as he got better." She dabs a tear. "We both knew he was kidding. He wasn't gonna get better."

"You witnessed Gerald leaving Orson's room the night he died?"

She nods. "Yes."

"Did you ever see Gerald around another patient named Kevin Huang?"

Tatianna thinks. "Not personally, but Nellie might have. She's usually there on weekends with him. I don't know that she'll talk to you though. She's been at that hospital for forty years, getting on close to retiring. She wouldn't risk messing that up. I remember that man, too. Huang. His whole family were lovely people. So sad they had to go through what they did. First, their son ends up paralyzed, then dies."

"Her witnessing Gerald leaving a patient's room right before he dies might be enough to get a warrant for the security video. Maybe they caught him going into and out of both rooms." Rick gives me a 'what do you think?' look.

"Both of those men died six or seven months ago," I say. "It'd be a miracle if the video hasn't been overwritten by now."

Rick sighs. "Good point."

Tatianna sits up straighter. She levels a heavy stare at us that, I think, has Rick swallowing. "I think Gerald could have killed those two. I mean, if you ever looked into his eyes, you'd know he could do something like that. They said Mr. Huang died of hypoglycemia. I know Gerald has requested excess insulin that wasn't associated with any doctor requests or patient needs. Ask almost any nurse at Teacup and they'll tell you that, too."

"This is extremely helpful," I say while still writing in my notepad. "Thank you."

"If the administration knows I'm talking to you about this, they'll let me go." She sighs. "But I'll testify if you need me to."

"Thank you. I'm sure the families of the deceased will appreciate you coming forward," says Rick.

"Is it all right if we contact you in the future should the need arise?" I ask.

She nods. "Sure. Why not? Either commit all the way or don't bother. My dad says that all the time."

"Not a bad philosophy." Rick takes a big bite of his sandwich.

While he eats, I continue talking with Tatianna about this nurse she suspects. Gerald sounds like an older man. She describes him as being later fifties or early sixties with white hair. When she describes his attempts to be normal, specifically that he tends to laugh at things that aren't funny but stays flat—or forces laughter—in the face of actual humor, I get the strong feeling he, too is suffering from mental illness. Either sociopathy, schizophrenia, or some form of mania, all of which can exhibit what they call 'paradoxical laughter.'

Of course, he could also just be a douche.

Mostly, I try to wrap my head around the fact that it's looking more and more like we have *two* killers at *two* hospitals.

So much for my luck.

Chapter Seventeen
Legit Haunting

My cell rings while I'm driving home that night. I answer via the hands-free. "Hello?"

"Hi, Detective Wimsey? This is Officer Lovell… we spoke the other day about that, umm, issue?" By issue, he means his ghostly problem, a dark apparition terrifying his daughter.

"Oh, yeah. I remember. Sorry I didn't call Friday. Been preoccupied with a case."

"Don't worry about it. I could've called you back and didn't. Figured you'd been swamped. Is there any chance you might be able to take a look tonight? Things have been getting worse."

Other than the current investigation which isn't keeping me here all night, nothing stands out in my mind as being pressing. "Sure. I can do that. I'm just on my way home now. Let me grab dinner and

I'll swing by."

"That works. See you soon, and thank you!"

I'd already texted Caius about being late due to meeting Tatianna. No reason to pester him with another message since I'm on my way home already. The rest of the drive is quiet, but takes a little longer than usual due to it raining fairly hard. When I go straight into the living room where he is, rather than up to the bedroom to change, he raises an eyebrow.

"Going out again?"

"Yeah. But not for work." I explain Officer Lovell having a 'paranormal issue' and asking me to check it out. "He said it's threatening his kids, so I couldn't say no."

"Well, let's eat and check it out together." He leaps up from the couch, gives me a quick kiss, and whisks off to the kitchen to plate our dinner—a portabella mushroom and asparagus dish over pasta. Another experiment with vegetarianism.

It's ever so slightly heavy on the garlic for my taste, but not enough to make a big deal over. Not even enough to mention at all, really. You know how men are… if I said 'it's a little strong on the garlic' he'd take that to mean I hated it entirely. Well, most men would. Caius knows me a little too well to jump to a conclusion like that, though the next time he made it, he'd probably skip *all* the garlic.

And no, it's not *too much* garlic. I'm just a spice wimp.

That's the Irish side of my family. My mother's idea of food is hours of boiling. Flavor was a privilege for people more worthy than us.

After dinner, Caius runs upstairs to get dressed, returning in a dark blue button down shirt, loose pants, and a black jacket. Honestly, I'm glad he's interested in coming along. Confronting dark entities alone is seldom a good idea.

I plug Officer Lovell's address into the GPS. He lives in Tumwater, on Grant Street. Since it's still monsooning out there, I drive. My pickup is a little better on wet roads than his sports car, and gets us there in one piece a little over thirty minutes later.

The house is a nice suburban two-story with an attached garage on the left. A row of spear-like evergreen trees forms barriers on both sides between it and the adjacent homes. Nothing looks too alarming from the outside.

I pull into the driveway behind a Ford Explorer, kill the engine, then dash to the porch in an effort to stay as dry as possible. Officer Daniel Lovell answers the door in a T-shirt and jeans, looking way too much like a normal guy. Not sure why, but I always find it weird to see patrol officers in street clothes. He also appears worried and exhausted.

"Hey, detective. Thank you so much for coming. 'Mon in."

"We're both off the clock. Call me Maddy. This is my fiancée, Caius."

"Hello." Caius shakes hands with him.

"Daniel," says Officer Lovell.

We step into an ordinary living room heavy on the beige. Big TV, couch, and a 'two kids live here' level of mess. The instant I'm past the threshold, a heavy sense of gloom falls on my shoulders. Yeah, there is definitely an entity nearby, and from the feel of it, a strong one.

Speaking of kids, the two children on the sofa look up at us. The girl's about seven or eight, dark brown hair and huge hazel eyes. She's terrified, but not of us. Her brother appears to be twelve or so, with shoulder-length black hair—which surprises me. Most cops I've run into tend to be hyper-masculine. Long hair on a boy is usually unthink-able. My father would've blown a gasket—but I think the kid's cute. He doesn't seem quite as scared as the girl, but definitely on edge.

A woman hurries in from an archway to the kitchen. She's so my patron spirit right now in a loose shirt and sweat pants, though the way she's looking at me—like I'm their only chance of surviving—is a little worrisome.

"Maddy, Caius," says Daniel, "this is my wife Brianna, my son Marcus, and my daughter Skye."

The kids both wave.

Brianna pumps our hands. "Hi. Thank you for helping. I… never really believed in this sorta thing until it started happening to us."

"There's something bad in the house," says Skye. "I wanna go to Gramma's."

"I've been racking my brain for days trying to think about what you said… if anything changed."

Daniel hooks his thumbs in his pockets. "I haven't brought any strange objects home. Neither have Bri or the kids."

"Any new furniture, stuff from yard sales?" I ask.

"Nope." Daniel shakes his head.

"Anyone do any dark ritual magic?" I ask with a goofy smile.

Daniel snickers. "Nope."

Marcus shrinks in on himself.

I glance at the kid. "Now that's a guilty look. Play with a Ouija board?"

"No," mutters the boy. "I got some music from a friend at school. He's into metal, too. Said this album was supposed to be like a legit spell or something. The band is from Scandinavia. I can't even understand what they're saying. Ancestral Wrath."

Caius snaps his fingers. "I've heard of them. One of their albums, *Danse Macabre*, I believe, is rumored to be a Latin transcription of ancient Babylonian demonic summoning rites. Though, even if that is true, simply playing the music shouldn't do anything." He glances at Marcus. "You didn't happen to draw a bunch of sigils on the floor, light candles, and offer a sacrifice while listening to it?"

The boy makes a face like we slapped him with a raw fish. "Umm, no."

I laugh to break the tension. "Then stop feeling guilty. It's extremely unlikely that music had anything to do with it."

Skye stands and pulls down the neckline of her nightgown, showing off a fading bruise around her neck. "The bad ghost tried to make me stop breathing. I couldn't even yell for Daddy."

Daniel scoops her up into a hug. It takes him a moment to compose himself enough to speak. "She started kicking at the wall in the middle of the night, so I went up to check on her. The damn blanket had wrapped around her neck like a boa constrictor. Took all my damn strength to pull it off her."

Skye clings to him. "Are they gonna make the bad thing go away?"

"We're going to do everything we can, yes. I wish I could promise you it will absolutely work, but nothing with the paranormal is ever a guarantee."

"What sort of things are going on here?" asks Caius.

"It chucks stuff at me sometimes." Marcus pulls his T-shirt up, showing us a few bruises on his back and sides. "Batteries, TV remote, Mom's crystal horses."

"I yelled at him for breaking one," says Brianna. "Thought he made up stories… right up until I saw a plate go flying."

"Tried to take my head off the night after I asked you for help," says Daniel. "Pretty sure it knew."

"Does that mean it's afraid of her?" asks Marcus.

"Where's your hat?" asks Skye. "You're supposed to be a witch."

Caius flashes a rogue's smile at her and winks. "We stopped wearing those about 200 years ago."

She giggles.

"Creatures like this are seldom afraid of anything really," I say. "It's more likely annoyed that I might be able to banish it from this house so it can no longer torment you."

We sit and talk for a while as they tell us about various events. Everyone in the family has been pushed down the stairs at least once. It's become so common that the kids have gotten into the habit of sitting and scooting from step to step to go down and crawling on all fours to go up. Both kids absolutely refuse to go into the basement, and Skye thinks the monster lives in her bedroom.

She's been the victim of the most attacks. Once, she'd been flung bodily out of her bed hard enough to bounce off the ceiling. Brianna starts crying at that story, asking me why it hates her daughter so much.

"I can't answer that with absolute certainty, but several ideas come to mind. One, she's innocent, so it may take joy in tormenting her. Two, attacking your kids is the best way to hurt you and your husband. Seeing your children scared and in danger is far more emotionally taxing than having a plate break over your head."

The Lovells both nod.

"If you don't mind, can we look around?" I ask.

"Sure." Daniel stands.

He follows Caius and me around as we explore the house. Whatever it is decides to lay low since nothing shoves me on the way to the basement. Then again, I *am* wearing three protective amulets and still most likely have some charge left from Caius' protection spell he invoked on me a few months ago during the esbat ceremony at his mother's. The cellar is rife with dark energy, particularly the corner on the left behind the furnace and water heater. For once in my life, I'm glad to be wearing shoes so my skin isn't constantly in contact with the concrete. Bare feet are like an exposed copper wire to soak up natural energies. However, it's also a path for negative forces if the ground is tainted. And this basement is feeling pretty damn tainted. Against my better judgment, I approach the corner that's giving me the strongest feeling, crouch, and press a hand to the dull green-painted floor.

The instant my skin touches the frigid stone, a sensation like rope cinching tight around my neck makes it impossible to breathe in or out. I gasp and gurgle, instinctively, trying to clutch at the cord strangling me. My heart pounds and I get lightheaded, but there's nothing physically there and my fingers do little to stop the painful tightness digging into my skin.

Caius notices my distress after a few seconds and pulls me upright and back toward the center of the room. Once I'm a few feet away from the corner, the strangulation ceases. I turn and grab onto him for balance, too dizzy to stand on my own for several seconds.

"Caius…" I wheeze.

"Whoa. Are you okay?" He looks into my eyes. "What happened?"

I let my head fall against his shoulder and take a few deep breaths until I'm once again feeling normal, then lift my head to look at a bewildered Daniel. "There's a really good chance you have a murder victim buried under your basement. Right here in this corner, in fact."

Caius gives me another look over, and seems satisfied I'm fine, which I am. He says, "How lucky then that there's an actual homicide detective here already."

"Right." I take in some ragged air, then exhale. "Okay. Back to normal. 'Anonymous tip' should be enough to get someone in here with ground-penetrating radar at least. No sense jackhammering the concrete without more than a paranormal episode for proof. Who did you buy the house from?"

"It was a bank sale. I guess they would know who the previous owner was. I can check."

I nod. "Okay. Let's take a look around upstairs. I'd like to see Skye's room since the activity appears centered there."

He nods. "You think if there's a body here, it could be that spirit doing this?"

"Quite possible." I fast-walk toward the stairs. Gotta agree with the kids. I want out of this basement.

"Could also be a victim of sacrifice used for the ritual to summon the entity," adds Caius.

"This is 2019, right? Not like the dark ages?" Daniel chuckles. "That stuff really happens?"

Caius nods. "It's quite rare, but it does. Typically, the sacrificial victims are animals, not people."

"That's *so* reassuring." Daniel flashes a weak smile.

Once upstairs, I go room to room. The house looks pretty typical except for small gouges in the walls here and there from where flying objects struck. A noticeable presence lingers in the area, though it doesn't make me feel watched in real time, more like something dark is close by, dormant. While checking on the daughter's room, I discover a suspicious loop of electrical cable in the closet… exactly at the perfect height for a noose. Upon investigating, I discover it's attached to an old gaming system on the shelf above. My imagination runs away with itself, picturing the girl opening the closet, the spirit tripping her forward and… yeah. I pull that shit right down.

Daniel gives me an inquisitive look when I begin rummaging his kid's closet.

"That loop was hanging at a rather dangerous height." I set the system on the floor in the closet. "This entity is malicious. Your family should be extremely careful until it's banished. It feels strong."

"Aye," says Caius, glancing at me. "You might want to bring in the big guns, Mads."

"Yeah. That's what I was thinking."

"Big guns?" asks Daniel.

Caius smiles. "Big guns have red hair too."

I nearly laugh. "I'm going to need to prepare some stuff and maybe ask some friends to join me here and help if that's okay. Give me a few days."

"Wait. So you're not going to get rid of it now?" asks Daniel.

"Not tonight, I'm sorry. Heck, I'd still need to run home and collect the appropriate supplies. But… this thing is fairly strong. I'd rather not take the chance that attempting to get rid of it only makes it angrier. Entities like this can lash out if the banishing isn't strong enough and fails to take. Much better it works the first time. Which means, the first time needs to be done right."

"I'm inclined to agree." Caius nods. "Also, if there are remains in the basement, they should be removed before we attempt any banishing. If it has a foot in the door, it will be able to get back into the house."

"Okay, that's fine." Daniel nods. "Faster the better, but I understand."

We head back downstairs and re-explain the plan to Brianna. As soon as it's mentioned we're not going to get rid of the spirit tonight, Skye bursts into tears.

"I wanna go to Gram's! I don't wanna stay here when it's dark!" She zooms off the couch and grabs onto her mother. "Please. I'm scared!"

Marcus looks frightened, but abruptly goes

blank-faced. "Holy shit. I mean, crap. You're Caius Craven!"

Daniel looks confused. Brianna gasps at the boy's language.

Caius smiles. "I've been accused of worse."

"I'm missing something," says Daniel.

"Dad!" Marcus jumps up and down. "He's the producer for like *all* the bands that don't suck eggs."

That gets Caius laughing. "Well, not sucking eggs is one of the requirements for signing with my label."

He and the boy spend a while talking about Hodeskalle and Is Drage, two bands he produces for. They're both from Norway and not exactly huge in the US except among fans of Viking metal. The conversation seems to calm him down, though Skye hasn't stopped trembling since learning no banishing would occur tonight.

Eventually, I assure Daniel that I'm going to put in a request to get a tech crew out here to run some GPR over the basement floor.

"Maybe the radar guy will unearth something worth looking *deeper* into," says Caius.

Daniel and I both groan.

"I'll try to arrange everything as quickly as possible," I say. "Hang in there for the time being and be careful for accidents."

Daniel and Brianna both nod.

Skye appears on the verge of a panic attack.

"This may sound strange, but if you want, I can

whip up some protection amulets for you tonight. It's not the same as a banishing, but they should make it less dangerous. I'd just need some hair from everyone. Not a lot, like plucked from a brush would be fine."

"Hair?" asks Brianna.

"Something to connect the protection to the person wearing it will greatly strengthen the effect. I could work with blood too, but that's icky, I don't have bottles with me, and I'm sure you'd prefer not to prick your kids."

Daniel raises a hand. "I'd prefer not to be pricked, either."

"Let her make the amulet thingies, Daddy," says Skye. "She feels tingly."

Caius sneakily pats me on the butt so the kids don't notice. "That she does."

I manage not to *eep*, and maintain a straight face.

"Tingly?" asks Brianna.

"Sometimes, children can pick up on those who have a true gift," says Caius.

Brianna takes in a lot of air. "Okay… if it helps. Be right back. Danny, can you help?"

Daniel heads off to the kitchen. A few minutes later, they return with four Ziploc bags, labeled with names. Each one contains hair plucked from brushes… except one. Daniel's baggie has much shorter hairs, almost like a bit of silt at the bottom.

"Sorry… I hope that works. My hair's way short."

"It's fine. I can make this work. Pop over to my desk tomorrow and I'll give you the amulets."

"Sounds good."

"Can we go to Gram's tonight?" whispers Skye.

"It's pouring rain," says Brianna. "Look, you guys can sleep in the bed with us if you want."

The kids appear to accept that as a decent compromise.

Caius and I head out, dashing through the downpour to my truck. We jump in, slam the doors, and wipe rainwater off our faces.

"Nasty one in there," says Caius. "I'd feel much more confident with the whole coven being involved. One of us doing this alone or just the two of us could easily pick it up as an attachment and bring it home."

I start the engine. "Agreed. Let's talk to your mother... *After* that body's out of there."

Chapter Eighteen
Reasons of Liability

When we get home, I hop in the shower to warm the chilly day out of my bones.

While air-drying, I call Abigail and fill her in on the issue at Daniel Lovell's house. "I think it's the spirit of someone who was murdered on the property. The kids are both terrified. I'm thinking it would be much better not to take chances. How do you feel about having everyone involved to help get rid of this thing?"

"Absolutely," says Abigail. "Do you have any information who they were? And when would you like to perform the banishment?"

"Not yet, and the sooner the better. There's a chance the remains are still on the property, so we should at least deal with that, first. Much more difficult to banish a spirit away from its remains.

I'm going to requisition a GPR crew to check the spot. If they find remains down there, we'll need to get the body out before we attempt to purge the entity."

"Quite true. Do try and find out the name of the person as that will help strengthen the invocation."

I bite my lip. She knows I know that, but she likes sounding like a teacher so I never protest when she talks like I'm a baby witch. Maybe she's thinking I forgot since I didn't mention not having a name? I adore her either way. "Right. I'll try to find out if I can."

"All right. I'll let the others know to prepare. Be safe, Maddy."

"You too. Blessed be."

After we hang up, I head downstairs where Caius is doing an impression of Venus on the couch... if she were a man. I swear he's part Satyr. Allergic to clothing. Then again, I'm one to talk at the moment. We cuddle together, sharing a blanket and basking in each other's warmth while sorta-watching a movie. Something about grey wolves chasing a guy in the woods. Not really paying too much attention to the screen...

***

I feel proud of myself for not staying up too late.

Tuesday morning, I'm not a zombie when I arrive at the station. A few quick phone calls—and some luck—gets Greer to sign off on a ground-penetrating radar crew going out to the Lovell's house. I attribute the ease partially to her knowing how accurate my hunches can be and partially to it being the home of a fellow cop.

Rick does me a solid and starts making phone calls trying to chase down the history of that property. If the radar people *do* discover a body, the investigation is going to be ours anyway, so we may as well start it. As they say, kick a hornet's nest, it's your ass that gets stung. If a homicide detective stumbles across a murder victim inside their jurisdiction, only a true douche would try to hand the case off on someone else. Barring something like being related to the victim, of course. While Rick does that, I call Vivian Prescott, reassured that she's probably received the fax with the warrant by now.

"This is Vivian," she says by way of answering.

"Hello, Miss Prescott. It's Detective Wimsey. I just have a quick question for you if you don't mind. I trust"

"All right."

"The suspicious deaths we were discussing the other day. Can you tell me if a nurse named Gerald Peters had access to those patients? Or if by some chance security video might still exist after this long that shows him going into or out of those rooms?"

"Hmm." Vivian hums to herself like she's trying to make up her mind. "I suppose it is possible. Both of those patients were on his floor, though I don't believe he had been their assigned nurse. Our security video wouldn't still be there after six months. We have a sixty-day overwrite policy unless an event occurs that requires preservation of the video."

"Yeah, I figured."

"Detective," says Vivian in an oddly cordial tone. "I'm of the opinion that Nurse Peters is quite likely reckless if not malicious. I've seen it firsthand myself, along with hearing the complaints. However, we don't have enough hard evidence to pursue substantive action against him."

"Is it a case of insufficient evidence or not wanting to deal with the lawsuits?"

Vivian chuckles. "Honestly? A bit of both. I'm having him watched as we speak, but so far, no new reports have come back of anything odd happening."

"It's quite possible he's aware of the monitoring and behaving himself for now."

"Perhaps. I will let you know if I learn anything more."

"Thank you."

I hang up with her and log into the computer. An email is waiting for me from Trevor Lauten, the pharmacist. He's sent me a list of names, everyone who he documented visiting the pharmacy the night he had the runs, as well as the drugs they requisitioned. Some are doctors, most are nurses bearing requests from doctors...

And Gerald Peters is on that list, requesting

insulin. He'd shown up at 11:09 p.m., soon after Trevor's shift started, likely when he'd have had coffee on the desk. I often start my day at work with a giant cup, as do quite a few people in the country.

I'm almost certain this guy spiked that coffee with a laxative, then returned hours later to break into the pharmacy while Trevor ran to the bathroom. No reports mentioned damage to any locks or windows, so either the guy has a key or he's also adept at picking locks. Or maybe they use badge swipes. Nobody is perfect. Trevor may have dropped or lost his badge at some point, enabling Gerald to somehow get and copy it. Or maybe Gerald snuck into the security office and got one.

I reply to his email and ask about the locks on the pharmacy.

"Got something." Rick drops a printout on my desk. "Officer Lovell's house formerly belonged to a Mr. Anthony Crowther. The bank foreclosed on the property in 1992. It sat unoccupied until 1999. The house sold twice more after that, once in 2000 and once in 2004. Up until the Lovell's moved in two years ago in 2016, it had remained empty."

"Wow. That's kinda telling. Three owners all bailed on it quick. What happened to Crowther?"

"He's missing. I found a police report when the Sheriff's office went to serve the foreclosure notice. Three men claiming to be Crowther's sons were at the property. They stated their old man went to Vegas and hadn't come back."

"Let me guess, he didn't have any kids."

"Oh, he did. Two. A daughter and a son. Both are on the East Coast. The Sheriff's office contacted them and confirmed the three people at the house weren't related to them at all, but by the time the deputies returned to the property, they'd vanished. They found all sorts of drug paraphernalia in the house as well as two young women who were near overdose, too out of it to flee with the men."

"And they left them there… how heroic." I shake my head. "You think those three killed him and buried him in the basement?"

"Possible. No idea who they were. Pretty sure they gave fake names. There's nothing in the file indicating the two women ever saw an old man there. Could be, they found him dead and just buried him so they could use the house for the eight or nine months it took the bank to foreclose."

"What is wrong with people?" I let my head loll back and stare at the ceiling. "And no, you don't have to answer that. You'll be talking for days."

He chuckles.

I spend a few hours looking into nurse Gerald Peters. His driver's license photo is unremarkable, if not a little creepy. Something had to be wrong with the camera since he looks like a wax statue. There's something just not quite right with his face. Aside from a slightly 'wrong' quality, he doesn't appear all that unusual or threatening. The DOB on his license puts him at fifty-nine. He looks like a fairly stereotypical grandpa type guy, slightly heavyset.

After some digging, I find he graduated in 1979 from the Columbus School of Nursing in Ohio. He appears to have moved to Washington State four years ago, but I can't find any record of employment that predates his joining the nursing staff at Thurston County Ultimacare Pavilion. Considering the crap he's likely been pulling here, I suspect he was dismissed from whatever hospital he last worked at—possibly with severance that he lived off until it ran out. However, Vivian confirmed that he works part time, only twenty hours a week on two ten-hour weekend shifts. That can't be enough to sustain an apartment, unless he's got a roommate. He's not quite old enough to collect Social Security, so maybe this is his second job. That would explain why it's weekend only.

I'm half tempted to interview Gerald, but also hesitant. Every bit of evidence I have right now is circumstantial. It would be silly to believe this guy hasn't been doing the same thing for his entire nursing career. The thought of how many victims he might've killed since 1979 leaves me speechless. Who knows how many states and hospitals he's been through over the years? Damned legal system. Administration is more worried about liability than people being killed... how many times has this guy been asked to resign rather than be reported to the police?

No... I can't tip this guy off that we're on to him. Not until I've got *something* concrete enough for a prosecutor to make stick. If we arrest him and the DA laughs at us and cuts him loose, he's going to disappear. Funny, I got the same feeling about William Johnston. Two angels of mercy. Two flight risks.

Goddess help me.

My desk phone rings.

I smile at the ceiling. Thank you!

Chapter Nineteen
When Good News is Bad

My phone rings again and I answer it.

"Detective Wimsey?" asks Amanda Sui, from the Medical Examiner's Office.

"You're like the voice of an angel. Talk to me." I grin.

She laughs. "Hardly an angel. So, I managed to have Lyle Winston's remains shipped back from the potter's field for further analysis. I'm about to send you the results. He was definitely poisoned via insulin overdose."

"You are amazing. Thank you! That might be enough to get a judge to sign off on an exhumation order for Patricia Holcomb if the family objects."

"No need," says Amanda. "I already took the liberty of contacting them with your concerns, and the family permitted it. I can confirm that Ms.

Holcomb died from an excessive dose of pancuronium bromide, also called Nembutal. It's an excruciatingly painful way to die. Someone definitely killed her."

I groan.

"What?" asks Amanda. "That's good news. It means you're onto something. Your instinct was right."

"Not really my instinct. We got a tip. However, it also means this case is turning into a giant mess. Turns out, I have a copycat killer out there. Then again, I'm not sure who's copying whom,"

"You're kidding."

"If only. Can you tell me more about Nembutal?"

"It's one of the drugs used for state-sponsored lethal injection." Amanda makes a faint noise of disapproval. "They usually start with a form of pentobarbital to knock the person out, then hit them with pancuronium bromide. There's some debate as to whether or not the victim feels it after the pentobarbital, but without that first, it's guaranteed to be agonizing. Imagine boiling water slowly winding through your veins until your heart feels like it's on fire."

"Thanks, but I'll pass on that particular fantasy."

"I have something else for you," says Amanda.

"It's veritably Yule," I say.

"What?"

"Oh, sorry. You'd call it Christmas."

She chuckles. "After we found Nembutal in Ms. Holcomb's tissues, I ran a check on our system for similar cases and got a hit. I knew it sounded familiar. It's recent, too. Only three weeks ago. The decedent, Shane Harvey, age thirty-three, was referred to the medical examiner's office from Oaktree Medical Community Hospital. They considered the death suspicious."

Shit. A *fourth* hospital? What the hell is going on? I whip out my pad and add the name, plus Oaktree Medical. "What do you know about his medical history? Was he a terminal case?"

"The autopsy indicated the cause of death as Nembutal overdose. Mr. Harvey had recently suffered relatively severe physical injuries consistent with a high-speed motor vehicle accident. There's nothing in here that suggests he wouldn't have recovered. No paralysis, no brain damage, only several broken bones and a lacerated kidney. This man should have been able to leave the hospital once he recovered from the accident."

Hmm. "That's definitely an outlier then. Might not be related, but it's too suspicious not to look into. Thank you!"

"You're welcome, detective."

I hang up with her. "Rick, we got another—"

My department cell rings.

"Wow, someone's popular today," says Gonzalez.

I fluff my hair over my shoulder. "It's the hair."

She chuckles.

"Wimsey," I say, after answering the phone.

"Detective? Sergeant Weber from patrol division. I'm at Danny's house. The GPR guy says he got a solid hit on human remains three feet under the concrete. How do you wanna play it?"

I glance at the clock… it's a little after one in the afternoon. Crap, so much for lunch. Or, maybe a quick burger on the way. I say, "Call it a crime scene and let's get the remains out of there. I'm on my way."

"You got it," says Weber, then hangs up.

"When it rains, it pours." Rick chuckles.

"Welcome to Washington." I stand, grab my coat, and point at him. "You drive. I need to call Abigail."

***

Eating Burger King in five minutes does horrible things to my body.

The noises coming out of my gut while I stand there in Lovell's basement are probably going to summon another demon. Neither of the kids have returned from school yet, though Daniel is home. He's technically still on duty, even if it's a bit questionable for him to be 'guarding' a crime scene that happens to be in his own basement.

Having Rick, three cops, the radar dude, his two helpers, and a work crew of three all down here at the same time takes the creepiness out of the air. I never did understand how that works. Being in a negatively charged place alone is *so* much worse, but with this many people here, the dark energy suffusing the area is barely noticeable. Maybe it's like radio interference?

I'm also not sure how the radar operator clearly gets 'definite human remains' from the bizarre squiggles and rainbows on the display screen, but the short Italian guy is beyond confident in his readings. Rick and I stand around watching a crew come in and jackhammer up the concrete floor. Let me just say that I *adore* ear plugs. They come in handy for smashing concrete in a confined space, going to the shooting range, and unexpected run-ins with someone playing Nickelback. I'd have said Justin Bieber, but I wouldn't use ear plugs there... that would be justification to simply shoot the stereo.

By 4:33 p.m., we have eyes on skeletal remains. Despite all the other people around me, as soon as the bones come into view, I get a bad chill down my back. This is ghost speak for 'fuck off.' My usual expectation for finding murder victims' remains is that the spirit—if it lingers about—is happy to be found, hoping that whoever killed them will face justice. However, I'm pretty sure this guy is pissed off that we're weakening his claim on the land.

Either Anthony Crowther was a bastard in life, or a brutal death twisted him into a vengeful spirit. The possibility also exists that the dark entity isn't him, but had been drawn to this place by the dark energy seared into the foundation of this house by what transpired here. Or maybe it's what compelled those druggies to become murderous.

I'm no medical examiner, but a two-inch hole in the skull is pretty indicative of a possible cause of death. Looks like a carpenter's hammer right to the temple. I put on the blue gloves, crouch, and pluck a small fragment of bone from the dirt near the skull, cradling it in my palm. Daniel squats beside me on the left, spotting a flashlight on my hand. Rick stands on the other side, snapping some photos of the makeshift gravesite.

My biggest question at the moment is if the entity here—and the remains—are who I think they are. While the other cops and the workmen mill around to let Rick and I examine the scene, I recite in a whisper:

"Restless spirit, broken bone,
"Here beneath your former home.
"Anthony Crowther, darkened shade,
"Show the truth that has been made.
"Restless spirit, speak to me,
"So I ask, so mote it be."

The bone chip in my palm stands up on end and flies forward as if flicked, landing back with the remains.

"Whoa," whispers Daniel. "Is that good or bad?"

"Mostly good. But not good." I swipe my hair off my face, tucking it behind my ear. "It means Anthony's still here. It's good in the sense that you don't have a demon problem. But bad because this guy's gone full dark."

"Why's he attacking my kids?" Daniel moves the light to the skull, laying sideways in the dirt, mostly still buried. "Wow. We've been living with a dead guy."

"I'm only guessing, but it's an educated guess." I lower my voice. "He's probably furious about being killed and having his house occupied by the murderers, used as a drug den and so on. As far as I know, sometimes, spirits can have a distorted perception of the living world, often seeing it as they remember it in their lifetime. Like a spirit from the 1800s still sees gas lamps in their house or some such thing. He probably reacts to anyone in this place as if they're the ones who killed him. Or, he's being territorial and doesn't want people in the house at all."

Daniel nods.

I stand, dusting my hands off. "Might as well get forensics in here and send Mr. Crowther to the coroner's office."

"Wow." Daniel whistles. "If I had any doubts about you, they're gone."

"Dad?" calls Marcus from the stairs.

"Don't come down here, son. Give me a minute, I'll be up."

"Yeah right. I ain't going down there, Dad. You know that!"

"Kid's got good instincts," says Rick.

"Hell, even *I* never liked being down here alone.

Always felt like I had someone glaring at me." Daniel blows air past fluttering lips. "At least it makes sense now."

I grab my cell phone to call in the forensics crew. "Gonna be in your hair a while tonight."

Daniel grins, rubs the fuzz covering his head. "That's okay. I don't have much."

Chapter Twenty
Doctor Rahman

Officer Lovell's basement does, in fact, eat the rest of the day.

It's nearly eight by the time we get out of there. Crowther's bones are on their way to the medical examiner's office, we've got a few gigabytes of digital images of the site, and the hole's already filled back in with dirt. There's no damn way anything useful to a forensics investigation remains in that house for a crime committed in 1992. The murder weapon, if it is a hammer, probably went out in the trash or got tossed in the woods decades ago.

The sheriff's report mentioned three males in their younger twenties who claimed to be Crowther's sons. They're probably still alive, assuming drugs or violence didn't kill them. But without photos or fingerprints, and only false names to go on, figuring out who murdered this guy would only be possible with magic. And, short of a highly unlikely confession, I doubt it would ever land in front of a judge.

Best thing I can do here is to throw out energy to the universe in hopes that karma comes around for these guys.

There's a chance that removing the bones might drag the angry spirit with it, but I'm not holding my breath. He's most assuredly attached to that property. However, with the remains off site, we'll be able to banish him. Otherwise, the corpse would have acted as a hole in the protective barrier he could've slipped back in through.

I fill Abigail in on the details, most importantly that I'm sure the spirit *is* Anthony Crowther. Invoking the spirit by name in a banishing ritual is the magical equivalent of stuffing a hand grenade into someone's pants before it goes off rather than throwing it in their general direction.

***

Wednesday morning, Rick and I head over to Oaktree Hospital to follow up on the information I got from Amanda Sui in the ME's office. Yes, a fourth hospital. So, I've got:

Olympia Health Services, where Kaitlyn works, the woman who first told us about this.

Saint Bart's, the hospital William Johnston

worked at five months before starting at OHS.

Thurston County Ultimacare—Teacup—where another suspect, Gerald Peters, is copycatting or partnering with Johnston.

And now… Oaktree.

I first approach a woman, Christy according to the nameplate in front of her, at an information desk, flash the badge, and explain we're investigating a suspicious death. Much to my surprise, she reacts with absolute concern and promptly asks me to wait a moment before making a phone call.

"Someone is on their way down to help you," says Christy.

"Thanks." I smile.

We sit on a sofa nearby for a few minutes. Eventually, an older man with Middle Eastern features walks in and heads straight over to us. Grey has crept into his otherwise black hair over his ears. He's dressed like a corporate executive in a nice suit, but has a photo ID badge hanging from a lanyard around his neck.

"Detectives?" asks the man.

We stand. "Yes." I introduce myself, then Rick.

"Pleasure to meet you. I am Dr. Ahmad Rahman, VP of operations here at Oaktree. I understand you have questions regarding a patient's death on site?"

"That's correct. We think it may be related to several other deaths in hospitals in the Olympia area."

His expression goes grim. "That is not good.

Please, join me in my office. I will do my best to answer your inquiries."

We follow him down a hall to an elevator, then down another hall into an area of nice conference rooms and offices, past an assistant's desk, and into his personal office. It's smaller than I expected, but nice. What is it with doctors and having shelves full of weird random things? Tiny globes, little statues of body parts, rocket ships...

"Please, make yourselves comfortable." Dr. Rahman gestures at four chairs facing his desk, then sits behind it. "How can I help?"

"A patient here died unexpectedly roughly two weeks ago. The man's name was Shane Harvey. What can you tell us about him?"

Dr. Rahman leans closer to a computer monitor —that doesn't retract into his desk—and spends a few minutes navigating the system, typing only with one index finger. Whew. Good thing this guy's not like a novelist or something. It would take him twenty years to finish one book.

"Ahh, here we are," says Dr. Rahman. "Mr. Harvey was brought in following a motor vehicle accident. It appears he suffered numerous broken bones and some moderate internal injuries. From what I'm looking at, he was in serious but stable condition and should have made a full recovery... eventually. His death was noted as highly suspicious and we referred the matter to the county medical examiner. Best to keep everything above board and all. We could have performed an autopsy in house, but in cases like this, I find it's better to be transparent."

Rick goes wide-eyed but stops short of saying 'wow.'

"The autopsy showed he'd been poisoned with Nembutal," I say.

Dr. Rahman winces. "That is horrible. Far from a pleasant way to meet one's maker. The drug paralyzes the subject's entire musculature, rendering them unable to move or cry out while simultaneously burning down their veins into their heart, eventually paralyzing the diaphragm."

"Do you have any suspicions as to who may have been in a position to administer an injection like that?"

He shakes his head. "Unfortunately not. If we did, I'm sure it would have been mentioned when we referred the matter to the medical examiner."

"Do you have a nurse on staff by the name of William Johnston or Gerald Peters?" asks Rick.

Dr. Rahman accesses another screen, pulls up an application, and one-finger-types each name. He frowns. "It does not appear so, and the names don't sound familiar to me."

"Maybe we've got a third suspect," I say. "Shane Harvey really doesn't fit the profile."

Rick nods. "Because Shane wasn't a terminal patient, nor was he elderly."

"Exactly. Most 'angel of death' type killers think they're performing acts of mercy. This guy was hardly a candidate for merciful euthanasia."

Dr. Rahman takes in some air. "I hate to admit it, but this sort of thing happens more often than most people realize, and not only in the US. A nurse in Czechoslovakia killed several patients in his care. A man in New Jersey is believed to have murdered something on the order of 400 patients before they caught up to him."

"Holy shit," whispers Rick. "Four hundred?"

"According to conjecture." Dr. Rahman nods.

"Hmm. So no dice on William or Gerald." I fidget with my hair while thinking. "Do you have any nurses on staff with a record of complaints?"

"Not that I am aware of beyond the usual ones."

"What about other nurses complaining to their supervisors?" I ask.

Dr. Rahman shakes his head. "If that has happened, it hasn't reached my ears. I don't imagine there to be anything left unsaid as we encourage people to speak up when something doesn't look right. You are more than welcome to interview any of the staff, provided they're not presently assisting patients at the time."

I nod. "Of course. We wouldn't bother any patients."

"Can you give us any information about Shane Harvey's next of kin? Given his non-terminal status, this could be a completely unrelated case. We'd like to rule out the possibility that he had enemies who might have come after him in the hospital."

Dr. Rahman turns back to his screen, clicking over to the first program. "It would be exceedingly difficult for someone to acquire Nembutal—or any form of pancuronium bromide—outside of a hospital setting. That drug is highly controlled. Though, I suppose someone with access to a prison's lethal injection stores might have obtained some. There's a contact number here for his wife, Jenna." He reads off the phone number. "I don't have any other contacts in the system, just the wife."

"Thank you." I jot it down in the notes.

"Perhaps I should also mention that there have been some irregularities with the pharmacy here. Some drugs have disappeared, but they're not the sort of things with any street value." Dr. Rahman traces a finger back and forth across his chin.

"Yeah. We've heard that before," says Rick.

"However…" The doctor lowers his arm to the desk. "The drugs that have gone missing could undoubtedly be used to kill."

"Which drugs?" I ask.

He again switches programs, taking a few minutes to review information. "Insulin, epinephrine, Nembutal, and digoxin." His stare hardens. "Son of a bitch… pardon my French. You're right." The man looks about ready to put a fist through his computer monitor, but holds onto his calm. "We have a serious problem, but I honestly have no suspicions as to who it could be."

I fidget with an excess of adrenaline and no outlet for it. So Johnston steals drugs from Olympia Health Services that Gerald uses to kill at Teacup. Gerald takes drugs from Teacup that Johnston uses at OHS. Though here, it looks like the murder weapon came from the local pharmacy. Ugh. If this case ever goes to trial, the jury is going to hate us.

"Please, doctor, it's important to remain calm," I say. "Keep an eye on the hospital pharmacy, but don't make it obvious that it's being monitored extra carefully. If whoever it is gets the feeling the game's up, they could vanish and start this whole thing over again in some other city or even another state."

"Or country," adds Rick.

"Good point."

Dr. Rahman nods, then hands us a business card. "Please feel free to call me directly if you need anything. For the sake of our patients, we must locate this person with all due expedience."

"My thoughts exactly. Have any other patients here died under similar suspicious circumstances?"

"I do not believe so, but in light of what I've just learned, we will take a closer look at all deaths that occurred on the premises over the past several years."

Rick hands him our card. "Please let us know if you find anything."

"I will."

We stand, shake hands, and make our way out.

Upon reaching the car, I take the opportunity to bang my head on the roof twice. My hair fluffs in the way, padding impact. Thanks.

"We're getting somewhere," says Rick, grinning. "Cheer up."

"Are we? The hole's just getting deeper and wider... with more and more hospitals."

"That's still somewhere. Might not be the somewhere we want to be going, but it's somewhere."

"I'm going to somewhere you right in the somewhere." I shake my head, not quite able to laugh, and fall into the seat.

Chapter Twenty-One
Force Majeure

Might as well rule out anything from Shane Harvey's background as a motive since we're already out and about.

After leaving Oaktree Hospital, I drive to the address listed on his license, Hollis Drive in Olympia. We again find ourselves in a pleasant neighborhood, though the houses here are a bit smaller and plainer than Officer Lovell's. The GPS leads me to a one-story rectangle painted an odd shade of... either brown or orange. Not sure what it is. A lone tree sits in a ring of bricks at the front right corner of a sizable yard. The grass is barely clinging to existence, quite far from being over-grown. Looks more like the fake turf from a model railroad setup.

The left third of the house is taken up by a

garage door a little wide for a single-car but not quite enough to be a two-car. A black Ford pickup sits on the driveway with its left side wheels on the grass, presumably so whatever car is in the garage can get out. I pull in beside it and kill the engine.

A short strip of sidewalk connects the driveway to a recessed front door. Someone inside is watching TV, from the sound of it, I'm guessing a Japanese cartoon. I ring the bell. The TV noise stops. A minute later, I ring the bell again.

Motion in the window to the left draws my eye to a thin blond-haired boy I assume to be around eight or so. As soon as I look at him, he darts out of sight. Another minute or so later, and no one answering, I ring the bell a third time.

"Go away or we'll call the cops," calls a possibly teenage girl.

"We *are* the police," I say. "Are you two home alone?"

Soft thumps inside the house draw closer. The inner door opens, revealing a slender tween girl with sad blue eyes and straight blonde hair. She half hides behind the door, peering at us through the storm window with an expression like she's hoping we can rescue her from a kidnapper. Warning bells go off in my head, but they're not deafening.

"Badges?" asks the girl.

I gesture at my hip, as does Rick.

The kid relaxes. "Mom? It looks like the cops." She pushes the heavier inner door open the rest of the way. Her pink shirt with some kind of anime character on it is too big on her, enough that her hands are hidden entirely in the long sleeves. Bare feet stick out from the bottoms of her baggy pajama pants. "Why are you guys here? We didn't do anything."

A woman around my age walks up behind her, also blonde. Pretty obvious they're related; the kid looks like a younger version of her. "Yes? Can I help you?"

"Mrs. Harvey?" I ask. "I'm Detective Wimsey, this is Detective Santiago. I'm sorry to bother you at home. Would you mind speaking with us about your husband?"

The daughter gets this far-off look and shrinks back.

"Umm. I suppose." Jenna Harvey opens the outer storm door. "C'mon in. Pardon the mess. It's been a rough few weeks."

"No problem." I glance around the living room, noting a strong smell of slightly burnt freezer pizza. The place is a bit messy, mostly with toys and snack food wrappers, but it's quite far from the worst I've ever seen. No great swaths of mold or armies of roaches here. "This is pretty neat compared to a lot of places."

"Yeah, right." She chuckles.

The boy observes us from the end of the hallway leading deeper into the house. We share fashion sense, the kid is also in a T-shirt and jeans, though he's barefoot like his sister. He sorta smiles at me briefly, but keeps watching Rick the way a field mouse might stare at a nearby mountain lion. Jenna, too, shifts to the right, putting me between her and Rick. Okay, he's kinda imposing if you don't know him. Tall, big frame, but he's got an approachable face. Well, at least to me.

We step around an array of small action figures and dinosaurs. The TV screen is paused on a glowing silhouette of a female shape with fragments of cloth either exploding off her or coalescing onto her. She's holding a wand with a heart at the end. Never did understand those cartoons.

Jenna sits in a recliner, leaning forward, hands clasped in her lap. Rick and I settle on the couch. The boy holds his ground in the hallway. His sister remains where she was by the front door, watching us.

"So, what is it you want to ask?" asks Mrs. Harvey.

"We're very sorry for your loss..." begins Rick. "But do you have reason to believe anyone might've wanted to hurt your husband?"

"Hurt him? Or kill him?"

"In this case, kill him," says Rick, powering through the uncomfortable question.

She doesn't take long to think about her answer before blurting, "Yeah, I suppose."

Rick and I both raise one eyebrow.

"You suppose?" I blink.

"Well, I don't know of anything like specific. He didn't have particular bad blood with anyone. But, he could be a bit of an, umm…"

"Asshole," whispers the little girl.

I shift my gaze to her.

"Abrasive personality," says Jenna. "Shane didn't shy away from letting people know when they ticked him off. Got into fights sometimes at work. I suppose it's possible someone might've wanted to get him back, but I can't see it having been so bad they tried to kill him."

She's referring to the car accident, so I ask about it.

"Typical Shane." She leans back in the recliner and sighs. "Was a head-to-head collision with him in the wrong lane. Probably got stuck behind a truck or a slow driver, figured he'd cut around them and gun it—only there was a cement truck coming at him."

"Ouch," says Rick.

"Yeah, well neither one of them had been going *too* fast." Jenna taps her arm. "Broke his arm in two places, both legs, couple of ribs. Punctured a kidney or something like that, too. Doctor said he was lucky. No brain damage, spine was okay."

The daughter clenches her hands into fists, her eyes as hard as diamonds.

"Can you think of anyone in particular who might have wanted to hurt him?" I take out my notepad. "Did he owe money to someone? Maybe some gang affiliation when he was younger? Gambling debts? Any involvement with drugs?"

"No. None of that. Shane liked to drink, but he didn't touch any of that other nonsense."

The boy appears at the side of the couch, clinging to the arm and peering over it at Rick.

"Hey there," says Rick, offering a handshake. "What's your name?"

The boy—and Jenna—both flinch a little at his fast hand motion.

He stares at Rick for a few seconds before whispering, "Jayden."

I look at him, the girl, the mom... They're all wound as tight as stopwatches. "How were things at home?"

"Fine," says Jenna quickly. "Money's a bit tight, but we were doing okay."

The girl scurries up behind the recliner. "Mom, they're cops. Don't lie. You'll go to jail."

Mrs. Harvey's expression flashes from startlement to anger to guilt to fear in the span of a second.

"He got physical with you, didn't he?" I ask in a gentle tone. "Kids too." The boy flinching away from Rick's hand like that tells me he's used to being slapped around.

Jenna stares at the rug between her feet.

"Dad used to hit all of us," says the girl. "I'm not sorry he's dead."

"Christine!" blurts Mrs. Harvey. "Don't you dare."

"It's true!" shouts Christine. "I hate him." She steps out from behind the chair, approaching us. "I was gonna run away. Had a bag packed and everything. Only, he got into the accident the day I was gonna leave, so I didn't."

The woman gasps. "Chrissy... no..."

Christine folds her arms, oversized sleeves flopping. "I'm not gonna run off now. He's dead. Duh." She twists back to us. "He put Jayden in the hospital once. Broke my arm when I was ten. Mom's been in the ER twice a month as long as I can remember. I was gonna run away back then too, but I got too scared that he'd get mad and hit Mom or Jayden so hard he would kill them."

Mrs. Harvey breaks down in tears. "Why are you telling them that, honey? They're gonna think I killed him and take you away."

"But you didn't!" Christine whirls to face her mother. "Don't be a dork, Mom. Cops aren't assholes."

Jayden creeps closer, peering up at Rick like a human seeing alien life for the first time.

Rick slowly extends his hand. The boy stands there motionless as Rick gently takes his hand and shows him how to shake.

I try not to smile too obviously at hearing a kid who actually *likes* cops. Yeah, there's bad apples, but it's such a warm fuzzy to run into a child who knows we're here to help.

"Shane was all over us," says Jenna in a detached voice. "Any little thing would set him off. Chicken too cold, TV too loud, kids not in bed on time..."

Rick shakes his head, trying his best not to appear as angry as I'm sure he is. "Sorry."

"I know you think I look guilty, but it's because I'm happy he's gone and that feels wrong." Mrs. Harvey wipes both hands down her face.

Jayden crawls up onto the sofa beside Rick and pokes a finger at the badge on his belt.

"I thought about leaving so many times. Every time I didn't and he hit one of the kids, it felt like I hit them myself." Jenna pulls her legs up, resting her head on her knees. "I'm so sorry for that."

Christine hugs her. "Don't worry about it, Mom. I know he said he'd kill us all if you ever tried to leave."

Mrs. Harvey lifts her head with a gasp. "You heard that?"

"Dad didn't exactly know what whispering means." Christine looks over at us. "No one really knew how much he hit us. Mom hid it well. All my clothes are big and baggy like this so people can't see the bruises. The doctors are probably suspicious. How many times can a girl fall off her bike, right? But he'd take us to different hospitals. Never the same one twice in a row."

Rick distracts himself from becoming enraged by amusing Jayden with his badge. The boy studies it, tilting it back and forth to make the light dance across the gold and silver. A lump forms in my throat as I watch this kid try to process being around an adult man who isn't going to hurt him.

"Ho... mice... ide," says Jayden, reading from the badge. He rubs his finger along the bottom of it and looks up at Rick. "What's that?"

Both his sister and mother appear surprised, and stare at him. Christine appears on the verge of crying. Goddess. That poor kid. Probably doesn't speak much.

"Homicide," says Rick. "It means we catch bad guys who hurt people."

"Guess Shane was really murdered then if you're here." Mrs. Harvey wipes tears off her face. "Should I call a lawyer? Is it foolish of me to just let you search the place? Shane always said cops pick a suspect, then look for evidence to make them look guilty."

I cringe. "I'm not gonna lie to you, Mrs. Harvey. Situations like that *do* happen sometimes, but it is not the norm. And my partner and I most definitely do not operate that way, nor does anyone in my department. Your husband *was* murdered, but the particular method in which he was killed makes it quite unlikely you'd become a suspect."

Jayden hands the badge back to Rick and salutes him.

Rick returns the salute.

"I knew someone killed him. He was hurt bad, but they said he'd recover. It's not right of me to say this, but we are better off. 'Course I don't make enough to keep up with the taxes on this place. Been considering moving home to my parents' house. Really, I have no idea who would've been interested in killing him. He was a shithead, but mostly to us."

I nod, rapidly scribbling notes about the family

dynamic.

"God did it," says Jayden.

His mother and sister stare at him.

"I prayed for Daddy to get sent to Hell and never let back." Jayden peers guiltily at us. "Am I in trouble?"

Rick whistles. "Oh, man... No kiddo." He gingerly brushes the boy's hair off his face and pats him on the shoulder. "You're not in any trouble."

My intuition tells me this poor woman wouldn't have had the nerve to even hire someone to kill Shane. Her guilt and fear are more than likely due to her dread of being on her own after spending at least twelve years in a toxic, abusive relationship. And yeah, it is a little messed up to be happy about someone being murdered, but in this guy's case, she gets a pass.

I give her the number for victim services and suggest she take advantage of the couple free sessions they offer. Probably not a bad idea to bring the kids. Rick winds up playing action figures with Jayden for a bit while I talk to Mrs. Harvey and Christine. The woman's clearly not quite ready to handle hearing that her daughter almost ran away from home. I do my best to gently scare her out of that idea by hinting at where she'll end up.

"I'm not gonna run now. Sheesh." She gives me this creepy little smile.

For a second, I almost think this kid could've killed him. But... she'd have had no way whatso-ever to get her hands on the drugs used. Poor girl is just so traumatized she's overjoyed at her father's death.

Oh, the effed-up things I see on this job. I have to believe the Goddess wants me here for a reason. There would be so much less crying in my life if I simply stayed at home and took care of my plants.

I'm seriously going to see that little boy's heartbreaking stare in my mind for weeks.

At least he's safe.

We leave Jenna with a card and a request for her to call us if she thinks of anything else.

"I know you're probably not too concerned about us finding the person who killed your husband," says Rick, while halfway out the door. "But, we believe the person who did it is involved in other deaths. If we don't stop him, he'll keep on killing."

Mrs. Harvey nods. "I understand. Thanks."

He walks out and joins me on the porch. She closes the door softly behind him.

"Ugh. I'd love to get that guy alone in a room for an hour," mutters Rick once we're back in the car.

"Which guy? Harvey or the killer nurses?"

"Either." He chuckles. "But mostly the asshole responsible for making those two kids so terrified. So who do you think did Harvey?"

I start the engine, sigh, and throw the car into reverse. "I'm guessing someone on staff at Oaktree Hospital. Or someone who's clever enough to pretend to be an employee."

"Harvey only died two weeks ago. That we

know of only one suspicious death there doesn't prove it's a one-off. Could be, they're just getting started."

"Ugh. Bite your tongue." I back out of the driveway, stopping in the street. "Something bothering you about this?"

"The case in general or that family?"

"That family."

"Yeah, quite a bit."

"I mean…" I shift into drive and accelerate down the road. "Don't think that woman had anything to do with it, but she knows more than she's letting on."

"Got that feeling too. Daughter?"

"You don't think?"

"Did you see that look in her eyes? I guarantee you if they had a gun in that house, the man would've been dead years ago."

"Maybe. But how would a twelve-year-old get her hands on Nembutal?"

Rick leans back in the passenger seat, hand over his eyes. "That's the million-dollar question. But I don't think she did it. Big difference between being a killer and simply wishing someone would die. Kid was fixing to run away. If she had a mind to kill him, she wouldn't have been ready to flee."

"She didn't… run away I mean."

"Still don't think it's the girl."

"You're just a softie for kids."

He lowers his hand, glancing sideways at me. "And you're not?"

"Fair point. No, you're right. The girl, Christine, didn't have anything to do with it... but something's bugging me."

"Well, let's go digging."

"Good idea." I drive a little faster, eager to get back to the station.

Chapter Twenty-Two
Prisoner

Despite my rush, we swing by the Fish Tale for lunch.

Rick gets his usual burger. I get a fish sandwich. Love this place.

As soon as we're back in the office, I proverbially roll up my sleeves and start digging into the Harvey family. Sure enough, I find numerous records of medical treatment for the kids and Jenna. They had CPS called on them half a dozen times, but the investigations never led to anything. Ugh. That man had his entire family so terrified of him they wouldn't talk.

I also locate a couple of domestic violence complaints on Shane, dating back eleven years, but nothing since. Aside from that, he's got no criminal record. Jenna's record is squeaky clean as well. For sake of thoroughness, I want to check their banking records and phone history on the off chance she hired someone to take him out.

This process takes a few phone calls—and for Jenna herself to walk into her local branch and speak to the bank manager. She does this for me within the hour, and, once I've officially been granted access to her records, I receive an email attachment from the corporate office. Her exported bank records open up in a spreadsheet before me.

There are no suspicious withdrawals of money or charges on her credit card. A few years ago, police gained the right to search credit cards without permission or a warrant. Although I do have her permission, I didn't need it. That said, nothing of note on her cards.

When I had Jenna on the phone, we also made the necessary arrangements with her cell phone provider. Verizon, in this case, already has a window into their system for us, and I access it with a special one-time password. Once in, I start digging.

I soon notice that she abruptly started placing calls to an out-of-state number the same day Shane died. The number doesn't exist in her cell phone history prior to that day, then all of a sudden there's five or six calls a day for a week, then two a day for a week, still going on at least once a day. Most of the calls are between forty-five and ninety minutes.

The internet tells me it's an unlisted number in Wyoming.

Prior to the day of Shane's death, almost every call in her record is to a single number that turns out to be his phone. The occasional outlier, I trace to the kids' schools or dentists, or ordering pizza.

Hmm. Odd. If she was going to hire someone to get rid of Shane, why call someone so far off? Then again, these days, that doesn't necessarily mean anything. Could be a VoIP number, and those devices could be physically anywhere regardless of area code.

The situation is so bizarre; I decide to call the Wyoming number from a landline.

"Hello?" asks a female voice that sounds fiftyish.

"Hi. My name is Detective Madeline Wimsey with the Olympia Police. May I ask whom I'm speaking with?"

"You call me and you don't know who I am?" The woman chuckles. "What's going on? Did someone put you up to this? Is this a scam?"

"No, ma'am. I found your number in the calling history while investigating a case. Do you know someone named Jenna Harvey?"

"Are you really the police?"

"Yes."

"Can you prove that?"

"If you like, we can hang up and you can call in to the Olympia Washington police department and ask to be transferred to me."

"I think I will do that. What was your name again?"

"Detective Madeline Wimsey."

"All right, dear. If you are who you say you are, I'll speak to you again in a minute or two."

"I'll be here."

Four minutes later, my desk phone beeps.

"Wimsey."

"Hey, Wims," says the desk sergeant, Cridlin. "Got a woman asking for you? Says you told her to call in?"

"Yep. I did. Send her over."

He does. My phone crackles once.

"Well, well," says the now familiar female voice. "Seems you really are the police. Forgive my suspicious nature. So many phone scammers these days."

"Seriously. They're everywhere. I just got a call this morning trying to say my phone service was suspended for verification and they needed to check my credit card number."

She laughs. "To answer your question, my name is Doreen Pruitt. Jenna is my daughter. Can you please tell me why you're calling? Did something happen to Jenna?"

"Ahh. That makes sense. No, she's... relatively okay. I'm with the homicide division and we're looking into her husband's death."

"Don't bother. The bastard's in hell where he belongs," says Doreen.

"Shall I assume that he wouldn't allow her to talk to you? Is that why there's no calls to this number until he died, then every day?"

"I never liked the man. Tried to talk Jenna out of marrying him, but she had stars in her eyes. And yeah, he wouldn't even let her call home, convinced we'd convince her to leave him. And, he wasn't wrong about that. The bastard treated my girl like a prisoner. Wouldn't let her out of the house except to go to work. Blew a gasket if she came home late. Lately, she's been filling me in on everything, and if that son of a bitch wasn't dead already, he would be when I got done with him."

I chuckle. "My partner felt the same way."

"Is something else wrong that you're calling me?"

"His death is suspicious and might be involved in a bigger case. I just saw an unknown number in your daughter's call history and needed to check it out."

"Is Jenna a suspect?"

"Not at this time."

"Mmm. Jenna wouldn't dare have tried to arrange his death. My daughter was far too frightened of what he'd have done to the children if he ever found out she tried anything like that."

"I'm inclined to agree. It's just routine to check on things like that. I don't see her becoming a suspect in this case at any point."

"Good. She's most likely going to be coming home to live with us here. She's having trouble dealing with making decisions on her own. That man killed her in a way. Going to be a long time putting my daughter back to who she was at twenty."

"I'm sorry for your loss… and I don't mean Shane."

She laughs.

I say, "Thank you, Mrs. Pruitt. I gave Jenna a number to call if she needs some support out here. I really think you should encourage her to see someone professionally. She's dealing with a lot."

"I'll take that into consideration. Thank you, detective."

"You're welcome. Bye."

"Bye, dear."

I hang up and lean back in my chair, sighing at the ceiling. Yeah, Jenna's definitely not a suspect. Total dead end.

"Off the hook?" asks Rick.

"Yeah. Shane has to be involved with the other deaths. I just have no idea how."

"Another late night?"

"If I didn't have plans, yeah. But, short of trying to get a search warrant for Gerald or William's homes, we don't exactly have much to work with yet."

"Plans?" He wags his eyebrows at me. "Anything fun?"

"Wading into battle with a paranormal entity tormenting a cop and his family."

"Sounds thrilling. Try not to get any green slime in your hair."

I laugh. "That only happens in movies."

Chapter Twenty-Three
Preparations for War

By the time I get home, my frustration level has increased to the point that I'm considering pulling an Ed Parrish and screaming randomly.

However, the sight of Abigail's white Cadillac SUV in our driveway calms me in an instant. I park and hurry inside. She and Elise are on the couch, having tea with Caius. Colleen's boots are on the floor at the left side of the couch, so she must be in the bathroom.

"Is Tamika coming?" I ask.

"Maddy!" Abigail bounces to her feet and whisks me into a hug. "Welcome home. Tami is going to meet us there. She'll be coming directly from her job."

"Hey, Mads." Elise also hugs me. "You look drained."

"Case is frustrating as hell." I melt into the sofa. "Tonight's one of those nights where I just want to sit in a bathtub and soak until morning."

Abigail laughs. Elise smiles, but it appears forced, probably because she's never really had a frustrating day at work. She's been living at the manor ever since age sixteen. Four years later, she's still basically a teenager who's a little too mentally broken to handle the outside world. Of course, Abigail doesn't mind taking care of her. It's not like Elise ever asks for money or gifts or anything really except a roof, food, and not being alone. Though, she seems to be gradually pulling her psyche together now that we got rid of the dark entity she accidentally set loose.

Colleen emerges from the hall and hurries over to give me a welcome hug. Given her most recent scary attempt at a relationship, she's sworn off romance at least for a while, instead announcing that she's giving serious consideration to forgetting about men entirely and collecting about thirty cats.

Of course, no one thinks she's serious.

To take my mind off the killer nurses for at least the rest of tonight, I explain what I've learned so far about Anthony Crowther, the dead man found in Lovell's basement. There isn't any evidence he had messed around with magic of any kind in life, so it's a simple 'angry spirit' haunting. He was prob-ably killed by transient drug users who buried him in the house, and his spirit has chased at least three other homeowners away in the past.

"Since the bones are no longer on the property, this should be reasonably routine." Abigail smiles. "As routine as magic ever is."

"Which isn't very routine at all." Elise bites her lip. "Thanks for still trusting me."

"Of course, dear." Abigail threads an arm around her and pulls her into a hug. "You're one of us now. Besides, you learned from the mistakes of youth. I don't imagine you'd ever repeat that."

"No way." Elise shakes her head rapidly, tossing her platinum blonde hair all over.

That girl's going to break her neck doing that one of these days.

I call Daniel to make sure he's still okay to have us come by.

"Please tell me you're not canceling, Detective."

"Just the opposite. Calling to make sure it's still on for tonight. And please, call me Maddy when we're not on duty."

He lets out a long sigh of relief. "Yes. Absolutely. And the guy's pissed. He hasn't laid a hand on the kids since they started wearing those amulet thingies, but it hasn't stopped him from using projectiles. If tonight doesn't work, I'm stuck choosing between selling the house or Brianna taking the kids and going to her parents' place in Federal Way."

"I understand. We'll be there soon."

"Great. Thank you so much."

"See you in about twenty minutes."

"Okay."

I hang up. "The spirit is ramping up. I think it knows we're coming."

"Well then." Abigail stands. "Let's not keep him waiting. I trust you have the herbs in order?"

"Of course. Packed and ready. Hang on."

The box I put together last night is still sitting on the workbench in my garden. I check it over to make sure I haven't forgotten anything. Of course, I have sage smudges for everyone. Also, Solomon's seal incense, which we use to drive away malicious spirits. Angelica root, another wonderful incense that lends power to exorcisms. This particular batch of angelica, Caius and I charged and purified last full moon, so it should have quite a bit more potency. Next are two mason jars of dried black cohosh that we'll sprinkle around the house to drive off the dark energies. I also made four witch bottles to set in the windows, each containing more Solomon's seal, anise, rosemary, pokeweed, vervain and hellebore—which comes in handy for healing emotional wounds, but it is also helpful for banishing. The little tennis-ball shaped bottles will remain in the house, a residual barrier against Crowther should he decide to try returning years down the road.

Satisfied everything's here, I carry the box back to the living room and smile at everyone. "Have herbs, will travel."

Abigail shakes her head, chuckling.

***

Caius drives us in his mother's Escalade while she sits in the passenger seat, holding a small cloth bag and invoking magic over it. I was a slightly naughty public servant and kept a tiny bone chip from the remains. Abigail embedded it in a small effigy of a human figure she made to represent the entity occupying the house. She's presently charging the figure to be a stand-in for the spirit. Our banishing spell will target the object, and by proxy, the haunt.

We arrive at the house a little after eight at night. Caius retrieves the box of supplies from the back while I lead the way up the walk path to the porch and ring the bell.

Daniel Lovell opens the door with a wad of white cloth pressed to the side of his head.

I grimace. "Are you okay?"

"Near miss from a kitchen knife. Just a nick. Bleeding like hell though. Scalp wounds."

"Ouch."

"Look!" says Elise, pointing. "The windows upstairs are all black."

Abigail leans back to look, then glances at me. "I don't see anything, but it doesn't mean it's not there."

"He's angry." Elise shivers.

Oh, did I mention she sees things no one else can? Yeah, there's a few good reasons why Elise is mentally brittle. If she says the windows are black, I believe her. Also, it's not a good sign. Not good at all. Means the bastard is ready for a fight.

We all head inside. Brianna, Skye, and Marcus are sitting on the couch, the kids already in their pajamas. At our entry, they sit up a little taller, no longer hunkering down, bracing for an attack by random flying objects. They seem curious at the appearance of my rather motley crew.

Daniel blinks in astonishment at the size of the group. "Wow. You really brought an army."

"This is my coven, less one. But Tamika should be here in a few minutes. We're going to do all we can to make sure this spirit leaves you alone for good. This is Abigail, our matriarch."

"A pleasure." Abigail nods in greeting.

"Elise," I say, indicating her. "Colleen, and you know Caius already."

Daniel shakes hands with Elise, then Colleen, and nods at Caius.

Abigail looks around. "Would it be all right if we set up in the dining room over there?"

"Whatever you need to do short of knocking holes in walls." Daniel smiles. "On second thought, I'll do whatever it takes to get rid of this thing. Just look at the hole in my basement floor."

Chuckling, Abigail heads to the dining room. She sets her huge canvas bag down and takes out a rolled up cloth, which she unfurls onto the table into a four-foot square pentacle mat. I once jokingly called it her Acme Portable Pentacle, but she didn't find that too amusing. It didn't annoy her, but she missed the joke. Guess she didn't watch Roadrunner as a kid.

Caius sets the box o' herbs down on the table. While Abigail sets out candles and bowls around the mat, the rest of us take the sage smudges out of the box like duelists selecting pistols, light them, and begin cleansing this room to establish a clear platform from which to invoke. The Lovells cluster together in the doorway watching us. Elise keeps looking at the daughter, Skye. The eight-year-old hasn't let go of her mother since we've arrived and the poor thing has dark circles under her eyes. Never before have I seen a little kid watch the beginnings of a ritual with such a desperate expression of 'please work.'

The doorbell rings. Both Brianna and Skye jump and yelp. Marcus, the son, only pales a little. Upon realizing what the noise is, he kinda rolls his eyes as if calling himself stupid. He looks quite keen on talking to Caius, no doubt about music stuff, but has thus far managed to resist interfering with the ritual.

Daniel hurries off to answer and returns a moment later with Tamika Bowen, the final member of the coven. She takes a smudge without further ado, and the five of us move about the room wafting cleansing smoke while Abigail continues to set up the mini ritual circle.

We migrate out from the dining room, splitting up to smudge the entire lower floor. Abigail follows room by room, lighting a single white candle once we've cleared each area. She's using stubby ones inside glass holders, just in case the spirit gets the bright idea to fling something at them and knock them over.

Once the downstairs is cleared, we repeat the process upstairs. Abigail pauses to speak to Brianna and Daniel about the need to have a lit candle in the children's rooms for a little while, and wants them to make sure the kids don't touch it. The smudging is like squeegeeing away the dark energy and the candles are a temporary sandbag wall to keep it from flooding back in.

When we complete the cleansing of the upstairs, Colleen and Tamika go outside to purify the perimeter of the house while Caius and I hit the basement. Since the house has a pull-down ladder to access the attic, Elise volunteers as the youngest, shortest, skinniest, and most flexible of us.

The basement still holds a strong negative charge, much worse at night than I remember it from the other day. Yellow police tape cordons off the spot where they dug up the body, even though the dirt has been replaced, creating a shallow pit where the concrete is missing.

A metallic scrape from my right makes me dive to the ground without hesitation, not even bothering to look. Not a full second after I hit the floor, something clatters to my left. I glance over at a large hand saw that just flew off a wall peg from above a workbench.

"Goddess…" Caius takes my arm and helps me up. "Be careful."

"Yeah. This guy's got a rep for throwing stuff.

Notice how fast I hit the deck?"

He nods.

Something thuds into the floor above us fairly hard, like a dropped bowling ball, but no one cries out. So far, so good. I creep along the wall on the right, walking around the basement in a circular, counterclockwise direction, wafting smoke everywhere.

Cleanse this dwelling, spirits harken,
This house no longer shall be darkened.

The furnace kicks on with a startlingly loud roar as soon as I get close to it. My brain gets stuck between jumping back with a scream like a normal person, drawing my gun and shooting the furnace as a knee-jerk reaction to a threat, or getting angry for being scared. The collision of three simultaneous reactions has the paradoxical effect of me just standing there blank-faced.

Caius pales and mutters a few unsafe-for-work words, then adds, "Bloody thing is doing that on purpose."

"Aye, 'tis," I say in an overacted English accent, for no other reason other than to calm my nerves.

He squeezes my shoulder; he gets me.

A grape-sized nugget of concrete bounces off my head a moment later, with enough force to hurt but not to knock me down or cause any real damage.

"Ow. Son of a bitch."

Caius rushes forward to check me over. He picks at my hair. "Don't see any blood."

A tremendously loud crash comes from upstairs along with Elise screaming.

We both stare up at the dark, dusty ceiling. Even the spiders have paused to wonder what happened.

"That did not sound good," says Caius.

"I'm fine!" yells Elise.

We exchange a relieved glance and continue the smudge.

I make my way around the basement, repeating the chant over and over until we finish the circle and arrive once more at the stairs. Soon, everyone has all gathered back in the dining room. Elise looks okay, though she evidently got pushed down the collapsible attic ladder when she tried to leave. Tamika's bleeding from a small cut on her forehead caused by a rock hitting her in the head, too, while she smudged around the exterior.

Daniel appears worried at the escalating paranormal violence.

"It's a good sign." I pat him on the arm. "It knows it's time here is short."

He nods, wanting to believe me.

Brianna mutters about being exhausted and goes upstairs to bed. The kids continue standing in the doorway with Daniel, watching as we form a circle around the table. Caius shuts off the electric lights, leaving us with only candles to see by.

"Umm," says Daniel.

"The spirits can draw power from electricity," says Abigail.

"Cool and freaky," whispers Marcus holding his

hands up like a director's frame. "You guys standing around that table would make a killer album cover."

Caius grins.

"It's time for the ceremony to begin," says Abigail.

"Should we, um, leave?" asks Daniel, still hover over his kids in the doorway to the hallway.

"You are welcome to watch," says Abigail. "We have nothing to hide."

"Please, Dad!" says Marcus.

Daniel nods, looks down at his daughter. "You?"

"I wanna watch, too, Daddy."

"There you have it," says Daniel, smiling nervously.

"Very well," says Abigail. "Let's begin."

Chapter Twenty-Four
The Banishing

Our matriarch removes the little figure she made from its bag, sets it at the middle of the pentacle, then draws her athame. She walks around the table (and us) three times, opening the circle, then takes up her position at the spirit point behind Caius. One by one, she invites us to join her circle, and we each accept in perfect love and perfect trust.

She lights the incense. "This circle is now open. We stand in the presence of The Goddess, the elemental spirits, and Hecate, who we ask to guide this wayward spirit across the veil."

The candles all flutter simultaneously.

"Anthony Crowther, your time upon this Earth in this incarnation has passed," says Abigail, holding her hand toward the effigy. "We bear you no ill will, but you no longer belong here. It is time for you to return to Gaia and find whatever path awaits you." She nods toward me.

I light my candle and recite:

"We call upon powers old,

"Bid this spirit do as told.

"Crowther wax and Crowther wane,

"Cause the living no more pain,"

Elise, Caius, Colleen, and Tamika repeat my chant.

Something falls over in the kitchen.

Caius lights his candle and recites:

"Dark spirit here we banish,

"Essence lessen, essence vanish.

"From this place we cast thee out,

"Your hold upon this house we rout."

The rest of us repeat his chant.

A sudden, powerful sense of dire warning grips me in time with a soft creak from the ceiling. Abigail must sense it as well, as she looks at me, nods, then 'opens' a door in the circle so that I may step out without disrupting anything. I nod and take a step back, turning toward the archway where Daniel and Marcus still stand.

No Skye.

The sense that there's no time to even say a word kicks me in the seat. I run out to the living room, then upstairs. At the end of the hall, the door to the master bedroom is open. Skye, as if in a sleepwalking haze, reaches into the nightstand beside the bed. She pivots to face her sleeping mother, a flash of metal glints from a small revolver in her hand. The child mechanically raises her arm, starting to aim at Brianna's head.

"Skye!" I shout, but the child ignores me.

I sprint down the hall, pouncing on the tiny girl and dragging her down to the rug barely a second before she can shoot. She doesn't struggle or cry out, her body limp like a rubber mannequin. I grab her around the chest with my left arm while keeping my right hand clamped on her wrist, pointing the gun at the baseboard in front of us.

"They are mine," says the girl in a man's voice.

Skye shudders and appears to pass out. The .38 revolver slips out of her hand.

I roll her onto her back and nearly yelp in surprise at the sight of what Elise must have noticed earlier: black vapors seeping in and out of her mouth with each breath. Shit. Her sachet amulet is missing. She smells like shampoo. Argh. She took the protection off for a bath and forgot to put it on.

She remains limp in my arms as I scoop her up and carry her down the hall to the bathroom. Sure enough, her sachet is on the sink. I hastily pull it on over her head, pressing the little bag to her chest.

"Upon this child your claim unglued,
"Get out, begone, I banish you!"

I repeat the words three times, focused on my desire to rid the girl of dark attachments.

The vapor puffs out of her mouth, so faint it's nearly invisible. She opens her eyes, scrunching her nose.

"Why am I in the bathroom?"

"The bad spirit attacked you, sweetie." I pat the sachet. "Don't forget to put this back on after you bathe."

She shivers. "I'm sorry!"

I hug her. "It's all right. You're not in trouble."

Skye's eyes bug out like she just drank a full pot of coffee. This poor kid is probably not going to sleep all night. I stand and carry her back downstairs, handing her off to her dad. He's picked up on the urgency with which I rushed out of the room, but appears to calm upon seeing the girl okay.

I hurry back into the circle so Abigail can close it properly.

She thanks the Goddess, Hecate, and the elemental spirits for their help and protection. Upon closing the circle, she picks up the small effigy representing Crowther.

"Anthony Crowther, you are banished from this place," says Abigail.

"Anthony Crowther, you are banished from this place," repeat all of us in unison, while focusing our energy at the tiny figure.

Abigail carries it out into the hall, and pauses to repeat telling the figure it's banished.

Again, we all repeat the phrase, following behind her.

She carries the effigy out the front door, symbolizing the spirit departing the house. At the end of the driveway, she sets it on the ground and lights it on fire. We form a circle around it, watching the flame consume the representation of the spirit. Abigail is an efficient witch… she's crafted the little guy out of pressed incense blended with angelica root and Solomon's seal. By the time the thing burns itself out, only a small pile of ash remains.

The bone fragment I 'borrowed' was so small— basically a splinter—it, too, has turned entirely to ash.

"Go wherever the wind may carry you," says Abigail to the ashes. "We charge thee do no harm, and fly thee quick to Hecate's arms."

We stand there for a little while more as the wind teases away at the ashes, blowing them little by little off down the street. Eventually, the sense of completion washes over us and we make our way back inside the house.

Nice… the energy in here is totally different. Elise perks right up.

Daniel and the kids are *still* standing in the archway to the dining room. As we re-enter, he looks at me. "Well?"

I nod. "He's gone. You shouldn't have any more issues."

"At least, not with that spirit." Abigail begins breaking down her setup and packing everything back in her bag. "An event like this does leave a permanent charge in an area which can attract other forms of spirit wanderers, not necessarily bad ones."

"Umm…" begins Daniel.

"That's why"—I hold up one of the witch

bottles—"I made these."

"A bottle of… is that sand?"

I smile. "No. It's a mixture of herbs and magic. There are four. Put one each in a window on all four sides of the house, preferably downstairs. They will keep malign spirits out."

"Okay." Daniel picks one up and examines it. "If it'll stop all this craziness, leaving tiny bottles in the windows seems like a triviality."

"It's gone," whispers Skye. "I don't feel scared now."

"She looks much better." Elise smiles. "It's not floating around her anymore."

Daniel swallows hard. "*What* isn't floating around her anymore?"

"Black stuff." Elise grins and waves at the girl. "It's all gone."

He nods, looks at me. "And what did you run off for?"

I nudge Skye toward Elise, figuring the 'kids' can amuse each other. Caius occupies Marcus' attention with music talk while I pull Daniel aside into the living room and explain what happened upstairs.

He about faints. "Holy shit…"

"Might wanna keep that .38 in a little lockbox or something."

"There's no way she should've known it was even there." He runs a hand up over his head, then exhales hard.

"You'd be surprised what kids can find. However, I don't think *she* did anything. The entity got into her. She doesn't remember it at all. Basically sleepwalking. But, you shouldn't need to worry about that anymore. He's gone."

Daniel shakes my hand. "Thank you so much, detective."

"You're welcome, but it's not only me you should thank. Everyone helped."

"Right." He smiles. "Is there anything I can do as a gesture of thanks?"

I ponder for a moment. "Mead and brownies work."

"We're witches, not fae," says Abigail from the hallway, coming toward us.

"I'm with Maddy. I like brownies!" chirps Colleen. "The mead, not so much."

"Fine," I say. "*Coffee* and brownies."

"Bit late for coffee, isn't it?" asks Caius, hugging his mother.

"Another night then." Daniel looks around at everyone. "Why don't you all come by for dinner? Least I can do."

The idea goes over well. But for tonight, we head home so the Lovells can enjoy some long-absent peace.

Chapter Twenty-Five
Five Coffee Day

Thursday morning comes way too damn fast.

One moment, I'm lying in bed hating the mere existence of alarm clocks. The next thing I know, I'm sitting in my truck staring blearily out the windshield at the front of our house. Wow. That's not a good sign that I can't remember getting ready for work.

Hmm, the seat's kinda cold.

I peer down and realize I'm still naked.

Oh. That explains why I can't remember getting ready for work—I didn't.

Just went straight from bed out the front door.

Sigh. This is going to be a five-coffee day.

I'm so tired I almost decide to say the hell with it and not waste the energy it would take to go back inside and get dressed. That makes me chuckle.

Captain Greer would probably be more upset with me for leaving my gun at home than showing up at the station sky clad. I'm sure she wouldn't be too happy about that either. Wonder if I could claim a religious exception? Then again, my coven doesn't adhere strictly to Gardnerian tradition, which suggests the power of the individual can be more readily accessed without clothing. Caius and I tend to agree, and have done a few rituals privately sans clothes, but the coven hasn't. Tamika's a little uncomfortable about the idea and Colleen thinks it will attract fae... which she doesn't necessarily mind.

Again, I sigh at myself. Wow, am I white. Sun won't help as I'll just go straight from chalk to lobster. Ugh. Yeah, probably should get ready for work properly.

With a groan, I shove the door open and trudge back inside. Caius, presently wearing the same outfit I am, stands in the kitchen by the coffee machine, chuckling at me.

"I was just about to go out and get you. Wondering how long it would take you to realize you forgot something."

"How damn late did we stay up last night?"

"Only 'till two."

I rub my face and groan. Used to be, I could stay up all hours and still have a ton of energy. That ability went away soon after thirty. These days, I need my eight hours or I wind up trying to go to work naked. Or something equally stupid. One time

I stood in the closet for ten minutes turning the doorknob back and forth wondering why the damn shower wouldn't start.

The oven clock torments me with the numbers 5:58. At least I won't be late.

***

I stumble into my squad room with a large coffee in each hand at 7:00 a.m. Starbucks calls it a 'redeye.' Basically, dark coffee with an espresso shot added.

… and I stop short in the middle of the area, aghast at cheap clown masks hung up *everywhere*. Ed Parrish appears annoyed, but I think Andrew Quarrel has gone around the bend, as he's wearing one and humming merrily to himself.

And yeah, I'm still way too loopy in my sleep-deprived brain to think about much, so I wind up standing next to Parrish's desk and talking while working on my coffee. Their clown killer 'passed' his psych evaluation, meaning he's legit nuts and not faking. Still no indication what about clowns set him off. They haven't discovered anything in the guy's past showing a prior bad experience. But he reacts to clowns like most people react to giant hairy spiders—wants to smash one as soon as he sees them.

"That guy's gonna love movie night at the prison when they show *It,*" says Rick, walking up behind me.

I whistle, shaking my head.

Quarrel cackles.

"Um, you feeling okay, Andrew?" I raise an eyebrow at him.

"Yeah." He lifts the cheap kiddie-Halloween-costume mask off his face. "Just decided to stop caring about being serious for the time being. So happy this damn case is finally moving toward a close."

"Ahh. Yeah. Speaking of closing..." I sigh, trudge to my desk, hang my coat up, and plop down in the chair.

Time to deep dive my suspects. I had been hoping we could gather enough evidence to get a slam dunk warrant, arrest these two, and put the case away... but between lawsuit-shy administrators and nurses wary of getting fired, and these guys being slippery, that hasn't happened.

If we pick them up and the DA either declines to pursue based on weak evidence or fails to get a conviction, Johnston and Peters are going to disappear into the blue never to be seen again. At least not in Washington State. Who knows how many more people they might kill before anyone catches them again. No, I gotta stop this here.

On one hand, taking my time and being thorough increases the chances of putting them away for good. But it also means more people can die before we make our move. I can't wait any longer. Maybe something in their files will give me enough to have confidence in asking for an arrest warrant. Or, Rick might get one of them to crack during interrogation. I hadn't wanted to roll those dice before, since my paranormal intuition warned me off. But, there's only so much hand-waving I can get away with. So, we file the paperwork to get warrants to go digging. We get approved for phone records and bank information. The IRS is also helpful, responding to an official request for information. They tend to help out as long as we're not investigating tax crimes.

Being tired forces me to work more cautiously since I don't want to miss anything or make a mistake. For most of the morning, I dig into William Johnston and Gerald Peters as much as the Information Age allows me to do from my desk. I've got some bank records, all the information we got from the hospital warrants, which included resumes listing past work experience and schooling.

I find driver's license records for both men, neither with any citations. There isn't an awful lot of information online for either man. They don't even have Facebook pages... or Twitter. Neither one appears to be paying much for rent. Both have monthly cash withdrawals noted as 'rent,' but the amounts are so low they'd have to be sharing space. That at least gives me a glimmer of hope that there might be roommates we could interview. Maybe one of them has seen or heard something useful.

Gerald hasn't been in the state all that long. His most recent address is in New Mexico. Chasing that down leads me to a record of him working as an electrician, which he indicated on one of his credit card applications—which is beyond weird. If this guy graduated nursing school in 1979, what the heck is he doing working as an electrician in New Mexico?

Ugh. I have to be delirious from lack of sleep. It's as if they've been trying hard to stay off the grid as much as possible. Which stands to reason if they are legit killers, come to think of it. Though both of them have licenses, I can't find any record of vehicle registrations. People can get around Olympia okay without owning a car, but it's kinda weird that *both* of these guys do that. Then again, they're working part time and don't—from what I can see on their bank accounts and tax documents— have any other source of income. Car payments and insurance are probably out of their grasp.

Which doesn't make sense either. If they worked full time, they'd be fine. Gerald isn't collecting Social Security yet at fifty-nine. He's still got a few years to go. So why wouldn't he be full time? There I go trying to understand why someone not in their right mind is making bizarre decisions. Sure it's a bit of an assumption on my part regarding their mental state, but well-balanced people don't become serial killers.

Ugh. I need a refill.

I drag myself out of the squad room and down the hall to the giant coffee vending machine. While I'm standing there waiting for it to brew, a clown pops up in my face with a growl.

"Gah!" I jump left, away from it, nearly falling as I stagger into the wall, clutching my chest.

Rick lifts the plastic mask up off his face, grinning like a fool.

When I catch my breath, I smack his arm. "Such an idiot."

"Sorry, couldn't resist." He tosses the mask aside. "I found something though. Maybe that'll make up for my idiocy. Check it out after you're done changing your pants."

I smirk. "You didn't scare me *that* bad. What is it?"

The coffee machine gurgles as it fills the paper cup.

"I think I found another victim."

That wakes me up more than the smell of coffee. "Dammit. Show me." I grab the cup and hurry after him back to his desk.

He gestures at the file on the screen.

It's a coroner's report for a man named Robbie Potrero, who passed away at the South Seattle Community Medical Center. The hospital considered the death suspicious, so they referred it to the medical examiners. According to the coroner's report, the cause of death is homicide via 'coronary distress brought on by an intentional overdose of digoxin.'

"Damn… it's in Seattle." I stare into my coffee. "And that's hospital number five."

"There's better news." Rick reaches past my side to get to his mouse, then clicks onto another window that overlays the medical report. "Employee roster. Gerald Peters happened to work there when Mr. Potrero died last year."

"Goddess bless." I lean back, trying to rub sleep out of my forehead. "Let me ask Greer to call ahead for us and smooth it over with the Seattle PD."

He nods. "I'll drive."

"Damn straight. I may ask you to give me a ride home later, too."

"That tired?"

"More."

"You witches keep odd hours."

"Such an idiot. Let's go."

Chapter Twenty-Six
His Name was Robert Potrero

One second, I'm getting into our sedan, the next, Rick jostles me awake.

Yeah, I slept on the drive. Amazing how much a quick power nap can help. I'm finally feeling energized. That said, I'm so going to bed early tonight.

We meet a pair of Seattle PD homicide detectives at the hospital's main entrance. A woman a little younger than me with straight brown hair and a sharp navy skirt suit shakes our hands. "I'm Detective Kennedy Clarke, and this is my partner, Detective Ashok Patel."

The man grins broadly while shaking our hands. "Welcome to Seattle. So, we understand our cases might overlap?"

"Seems that way..." I explain what I know

about our suspects, Johnston and Gerald as well as the other mysterious deaths on the way inside and down the hall.

By the time we reach the office of an administrator who's willing to talk to us, Detectives Clarke and Patel share my belief that what happened here was the work of Gerald Peters.

Doctor Natalie Roth, director of patient services, instantly hits me with 'bitch vibes.' She's gotta be in her early sixties, pewter grey hair up in a bun, and has a look of stern seriousness about her—right up until she introduces herself. At that point, the strict 'teacher from hell' persona I imagined evaporates to a pleasant smile riding upon a layer of professionalism.

"Welcome, detectives. Please, sit and let me know what brings you here."

"We're looking for information regarding a suspicious death that occurred on the premises," says Detective Clarke. "The deceased is Robbie Potrero." She reads off his former social security number.

Dr. Roth nods, accesses her computer, and reads for a little while. "Hmm. Mr. Potrero was rushed here after suffering an injury at his job. The man worked as an electrician for Puget Sound Energy. According to our records, he sustained a massive shock at a substation yard and had already lost consciousness by the time he arrived here." She winces. "Both of his arms vaporized. He lost his jaw, eyes, and most of his left leg."

"Holy shit," mumbles Rick.

I squirm in my chair at the thought. "Was he expected to survive otherwise?"

"It's difficult to say based on this." Dr. Roth scrolls the file, reading. "It's a miracle he lived at all. Most people who suffer an electrical shock of that magnitude are dead in an instant. He'd been in ICU for not even a full twenty-four hours before he coded. Had he made it through the first forty-eight hours, his odds of survival would've become drastically better. In my opinion, Mr. Potrero would most likely have passed away within a week or two given the severity of his injuries. Much of his internal tissues experienced thermal damage. He was surely headed for renal failure, and quite possibly systemic shock. While it isn't unexpected for a patient in his condition to suffer cardiac arrest, we did discover that he had been given an injection of digoxin sufficient enough to hasten his death."

"Does the hospital have any suspicions as to where that dose came from?" asks Detective Patel.

Dr. Roth clicks her mouse a few times while reading her screen. "According to our records, Mr. Potrero passed away over a year ago. There is one name that comes to mind. Our doctors and head nurses brought it to the administration's attention. Gerald Peters."

Detective Clarke looks over an iPad. "We looked into that, but the HR person—Ron Larson— didn't give us too much."

Hmm. That makes me feel old school for using

an actual paper and pen to take notes. But I write a *lot* faster than I can type on a touch screen. And paper notepads don't run out of battery power. Rick seems to have notepad envy, but I doubt he's going to push Greer to get us iPads. Cops are like cats. We hate change.

Dr. Roth nods once. "We haven't had any similar cases since that death, fortunately. Coincidentally—or not—Nurse Peters was dismissed soon after that case and has not been back."

"What can you tell us about him?" I ask.

"One moment." Dr. Roth stares at her computer for a little while, her face aglow in the shifting light from multiple windows opening and closing. "He worked here from September 2015 to June of 2017."

"Part time or full?" I ask.

"Part," says Dr. Roth, still paging down the file. "Weekends only."

"Did you two talk to Peters?" asks Rick, looking at the Seattle detectives.

"We caught up with him at, oh what was it?" Detective Clarke swipes at her iPad. "Thurston County Ultimacare. The guy seemed a bit off."

"Something about him did not feel right." Detective Patel shakes his head. "But we had no real evidence. And the man may simply have been highly uncomfortable around people."

"Great quality for a nurse to have," says Rick.

"Indeed." Detective Patel glances at his iPad. "We watched him for a few weeks, but nothing came of it."

Dr. Roth leans back in her chair. "Despite the administration implicating Peters in the death of Mr. Potrero, the police declined to prosecute him, citing insufficient evidence."

Detective Clarke shoots a deadly look off to the side while Patel seems apologetic.

"The DA wouldn't pursue charges with the evidence we had," says Detective Clarke. "We had no choice but to cold case the investigation for the time being. However... in light of the new information you're bringing into this, I'm going to pull this case to the top of the list."

"Indeed." Patel starts tapping furiously on his iPad. "We should share whatever we can."

"Good call." Rick pretends to type on his paper notepad. "I'll email our half to you guys as soon as we're back in the office."

"So what happened to Peters here?" I ask.

Dr. Roth frowns. "Ultimately, we let him go for chronic lateness as well as showing up to work drowsy to the point other nursing staff suspected him of being intoxicated."

Feeling somewhat guilty of that myself, I sit up straighter.

"That's a big part of what scared the DA off," says Patel. "Peters' record of chronic fatigue cast too much doubt and the DA thought the jury would attribute the death to an accident caused by sleep deprivation and carelessness."

"Indeed," says Dr. Roth. "We settled with Mr.

Potrero's family. No lawsuits have been filed in the matter."

Wow, this guy just keeps catching breaks. I make a note in my file, and underline *lucky bastard*.

Rick asks, "At the time Mr. Peters worked here, did your hospital pharmacy report any medicines missing?"

Dr. Roth checks the computer. "Yes. There had been several irregularities with the pharmacy during that period. A month or two after Mr. Peters was dismissed, we discovered that he had used falsified requisition orders on at least four occasions to request insulin, epinephrine, and digoxin."

"Why wasn't that mentioned to us?" asks Detective Clarke.

"It should have been." Dr. Roth clicks a few keys. "There is a note in here that shows we mailed the documents to you August 9, 2017."

Both Clarke and Patel appear frustrated. Some-times, police station mailrooms can be a vortex of doom. One inattentive clerk stashes one envelope somewhere 'for later,' and there it sits.

"Can you please re-send that?" asks Detective Clarke.

"Of course." Dr. Roth leans forward, types for a bit and clicks the mouse. A printer on the side of the office whirs to life. "May as well just hand it to you since you're here. Printing two copies."

"Thank you." Detective Patel walks over to the printer and returns sifting documents. He separates the stack into two piles and hands me one.

"Thanks."

He nods.

"Is there anything else I can help you with, detectives?" asks Dr. Roth.

"Can you point us at Gerald's supervisor?" I ask.

"Marlene Davies. She's not in yet. She's the head nurse on the night crew. Her shift starts at nine."

I close my notepad. "All right. That's all I can think of."

Detectives Clarke and Patel ask about any other patients who may have died under suspicious circumstances when Gerald had been on staff. Dr. Roth isn't aware of any, but agrees to have her people check over the records and look for any possible matches.

We thank her and leave. Rick has an odd look on his face like he's about to laugh at something.

"Rick, the man lost limbs! So help me, if you refer to his death as 'shocking,' I will legit hit you."

He cringes. "Nah. That's too dark even for me, but I'm not the one who thought of saying it. You just made the joke while pretending to take the high ground."

"Did not." I stick my tongue out at him, forgetting we have other detectives watching.

"I like you guys." Detective Clarke chuckles. "Good to see not everyone at Central's a stuffed shirt."

"We're tolerable in small doses," says Rick,

winking.

"The guy wouldn't have had much of a life if he survived," says Detective Patel.

I give him side eye, wondering if he agrees with Peters for killing.

"I take it Nurse Peters thinks he's some kind of angel of mercy?" asks Clarke.

"That's about right," I answer, pulling my hair off my face.

Rick sighs. "But we need to remind him life or death is not his decision to make."

"We'll start checking around here to see if we can find anything else that might help." Detective Clarke pauses at the exit to shake our hands again. "Thanks for reopening an old case for us."

I grin. "Hah. You're welcome."

"No. Seriously. This one bugged me. Kinda pissed me off that the DA wouldn't run with it. Let's nail this slippery bastard once and for all."

"How do you skin an eel?" Rick makes a hammering gesture. "Nail its head to the board first."

We all wince, but Rick has a point.

We got to pin this guy down, somehow.

And nail him.

Chapter Twenty-Seven
Not Quite the Whole Truth

We grab lunch on the way back and, still munching on my chicken Caesar wrap, I dive into the computer system again, pulling up all the records for the known victims from four hospitals and arranging them into a comparison sheet.

Patricia Holcomb, Lyle Winston, and Steve Abbott go under *William Johnston*.

Kevin Huang, Orson Gunn, and Robbie Potrero go under *Gerald Peters*.

I put the abusive Shane Harvey off to the side under a big question mark.

Normally, I do a board like this in an effort to nail down some common thread between victims and determine the killer's motive. I've already got the motive... or so I think. Mercy—or so I am assuming the two killers think that way. Question being: do Johnston and Peters know each other? What are the odds of two 'angels of death' operating in the same area at the same time? Drugs stolen from one hospital and used in another suggest the men are collaborating. Maybe they met on the job somewhere?

Okay, mission: find out where William Johnston and Gerald Peters both worked at the same hospital at the same time. If I can find some overlap, maybe I can prove collaboration. Johnston doesn't appear to have come from out of state, so I put together a list of hospitals in the area, sort by distance from Olympia, and begin calling around.

No need to call the hospitals I already know about, so I pass over them and start calling different places. I strike out at the first two, neither man having been at either one.

Before I can call the third hospital, my phone lights up with an inbound call.

"Wims," says Sergeant Cridlin at the front desk. "Got a call for you. Woman says you told her to contact you? Jenna Harvey?"

"Sure did. Thanks. Send her through."

My phone *beeps*.

"This is Detective Wimsey. Mrs. Harvey?"

"Hi. Please, call me Jenna. I'm going to drop his name and go back to using Pruitt. The kids want to do it, too, but that's going to take the courts to get involved."

"Yeah. Good symbolic change for you."

"So, umm… is it illegal to lie to the cops?"

"Depends on the lie. If you're trying to cover up a crime, then yes. If you tell me that you came from the coffee shop to conceal that you were hanging out at a strip club, that's not a big deal."

She laughs. "No, nothing like that. Umm. My daughter Christine has been pushing me to tell you something I left out. I've been thinking about what you said, that this nurse guy might kill other people."

"Okay…" I grab my notepad and flip it open to a blank page.

"When Shane was in the hospital, I took the kids and we went there to visit him after they got him set up in ICU. None of us really wanted to go, but we were afraid of how he'd be if he found out we didn't visit him."

"Right…"

"I guess it was kinda obvious something wasn't right with us. I mean, you and your partner figured out he hit us after what, five minutes? This nurse stopped in. Such a sweet man. It was almost like he could see 'battered wife' written across my forehead. Well, maybe that literally was true. Might've had a bruise or two back then." She sniffles. "Um, so this nurse started asking me if I was okay, if the kids were okay. I'd never ever told anyone before that Shane hit me or the kids, but it just kinda slipped out. This man made me feel so safe, like I could tell him anything. Jayden and Christine talked to him, too. My son told him how his Daddy would hit him all the time… and the man damn near cried."

I swallow the lump in my throat before it can get too big. "Do you remember who he was?"

"He never did tell me his name. But he was a nurse. That I remember."

"Could it have been George? Jim? Gerald? Wilbur? Walter? William?" I ask, throwing in a few decoy names so I'm not priming her to answer what I want to hear.

"I don't think so, no. None of those."

"What did he look like?"

"Well… he wasn't too old. Thirties maybe. Totally bald like a skinhead. He kinda looked like a biker."

I jot that down. Damn. That doesn't match either Gerald *or* William's description.

"Is that helpful?" asks Jenna. "I was thinking this nurse might be the one who… killed Shane. He looked at me like I was this little lost kitten stuck out in the rain and he wanted to take me home."

"Did he say anything to that effect? Ask you out?"

"Oh, no… I didn't mean it that way. I don't think he… well *if* he did anything, I don't think he was trying to get rid of my husband so he could go out with me. Just had this feeling like he wanted to save me from Shane. Honestly, I think the guy could've been gay. He didn't check me out at all. Not even a little."

"Well, not every guy is a total horndog," I say.

"I beg to differ," says Rick, barely over a

whisper. "Some of us can simply hide it while operating in a professional capacity."

I roll my eyes.

"Maybe," says Jenna, mercifully not hearing Rick. "But I had to tell you about that before I drove myself crazy with guilt."

"Thank you. This might be very helpful."

We talk for a little while. Jayden apparently believes that God actually killed his father, and isn't sure if he's going to be in trouble for asking 'the big guy' to kill someone. Christine is eager to go to Wyoming. She didn't have any friends around here, mostly due to how controlling her father had been. Kids at her present school all picked on her for being quiet. It's so weird to hear about a twelve-year-old overjoyed that her father is dead.

Eventually, we get off the phone, again with a reminder that she can call me if she needs anything.

I add 'bald biker?' to my crime board above Shane Harvey's name.

"Shit," says Rick. "Do we have *three* effing serial killers in Olympia at once? What are the damn odds?"

"Never ask that," says Detective Gonzalez from her desk. "Quarrel asked that once and now we have clown crap all over the office."

Laughter truly is contagious.

And sometimes mildly psychotic.

Chapter Twenty-Eight
A Little Reward

The fading high of carnal bliss gradually leaves my consciousness.

I'm lying in bed staring at the ceiling, wearing only a layer of sweat and Caius' arm. His rapid, hot breaths blast out of his nose across my chest. He's stretched out beside me, head on my shoulder. Neither one of us feels inclined to move.

The promise I made to myself that I'd go to bed early came true, only 'going to bed' did not translate to sleep. My whole body tingles; my nerve endings throwing off cascading energy like Fourth of July sparklers. I can neither move nor close my eyes. Well, I probably *can* move; I merely don't want to.

My mind drifts around in circles, daydreaming of our upcoming wedding. It's an occasion I've been simultaneously looking forward to and being afraid of before he proposed. Now that he's proposed, all the fear is gone and it's pure anticipation. Okay, not completely true. Some dread remains, but it isn't at all about marrying him, it's dealing with all the arrangements and other crap.

Those people who run off to Vegas and get married in an hour on the weekend? Yeah, they might have something there. I'm half tempted to say if Caius wants to make a big production out of it, he's free to deal with the planning. Does that mean I have to turn in my woman card? To hear the guys at the station talk, it's always the woman who wants to have a huge wedding and everything to be perfect and so on.

I just want to be Mrs. Craven, and don't care at all how elaborate or simple the handfasting is.

Caius toyed with the idea of taking *my* name, Wimsey. Maybe we'll hyphenate. Though Craven-Wimsey sounds like someone searching for a comedy. Names have power, though… so we might wind up not even changing them. So many people call me Wims or Wimsey it would be weird otherwise.

Eventually, my breathing slows to normal. The last vestiges of physical pleasure give way to a total emotional high as I bask in the presence of the man I love so completely. I close my eyes and try to let myself drift off, but my brain decides to pick that moment to start gnawing on the case like a stubborn cow chewing a wad of grass. Bald biker dude. Do we really have a third person involved? Is this like some kind of evil nurse cult?

Caius randomly starts talking about a band he's considering taking on, Gethsemane. Apparently, the lead singer is super religious. Most of their songs are heavy in biblical themes, primarily the battle between good and evil. He describes their sound and lyrics as more epic fantasy and not at all preachy, which is probably why he's considering signing them. That, and the music is pretty good.

"Yeah, surprised me, too. The lead singer, Randy, is a beast of a singer."

"Also, it's nice to see someone sincere in their faith, even if they only believe in *one* god."

I nod. "You know their god probably is real… but I don't think he's alone."

Caius shrugs. "Well they have that whole trinity thing, so isn't that technically three gods? Or is it somehow just the one? Three is one, one is three? Never did understand that."

No effing way. He did it again.

I sit up. "Thank you."

"I haven't done anything more…" He begins sliding his hand over my hip. "But I could."

"Eep!" I gasp, grabbing his hand—but not pulling it away. "You just explained something, but I don't know how you explained it."

"That makes total sense." He rolls his eyes.

Oh, his fingertip is closing in on a bad place. Making it hard to think. Wait, that's a good place. But… "I mean…" A gasp comes out of me. "It just hit me that maybe there aren't three killers. William's online trails are so brief and basic, Gerald's too. What you just said about the three being one set something off in the back of my mind."

I squirm. His finger is about to set something off elsewhere.

"Happy to help even if I didn't intend to."

"Cernunnos must've inspired you to ramble. And… it feels right."

"You're welcome."

"Not that." A shudder makes my legs twitch. "Well, that feels right, too. But what you said feels right." I ease his hand away and roll on top of him. "Someone deserves a little reward."

Caius wags his eyebrows.

So much for going to sleep early.

Chapter Twenty-Nine
Momentum

Despite only getting six hours of sleep, I bounce out of bed in the morning.

I'm shaking with excess energy by the time I reach the squad room. Rick's just taking his coat off, having arrived not a full minute earlier. He hangs it on the peg beside his desk and watches me zoom up to him.

"I think I know what's going on."

"Well good, because no one else seems to." He chuckles.

"No, I mean with the case."

A boisterous fart comes from Ed Parrish's direction.

"Gah! For shit's sake, who did that?" he yells, nearly falling off his chair.

Everyone stares at him.

"Change thine shorts," calls Rick. "That

sounded… full."

He recovers his balance, then holds up a whoopee cushion. "Not funny."

"*Au contraire*. That was hilarious." Quarrel smiles. "And no, it wasn't me."

Parrish chucks it in the trash. "This clown stuff is getting out of hand."

Rick and I lose a moment laughing.

I start explaining the theory that perhaps William, Gerald, and this unknown 'skinhead biker' are potentially the same person. While I'm in the middle of showing Rick the awfully small paper trails left by William and Gerald—it makes so much sense why they appear to be off the grid if they're not real people.

"There's an easy way to find that out," says Rick. "Let's come up with some bullshit reason to visit them at home, check out their addresses in person. Survey or sweepstakes or something, so they don't know the police are sniffing around."

I start nodding, but glance over at motion coming toward us.

A uniformed officer escorts a short, twenty-something black woman in teal scrubs over to us. She has an air of trepidation about her but also hopeful determination.

"Detectives? This woman says she has inform-ation you'd be interested in about a case you're working on." Officer Fuentes nods at me, then Rick.

"Hello." I offer a hand. "Detective Wimsey."

"Maya Britton." The woman shakes my hand.

"I'm an RN at Oaktree Hospital." She shakes Rick's hand as he introduces himself. "Saw you two poking around the other day. It's really good to see that you guys are taking our concerns seriously. Everyone on my shift is talking about... something that happened recently. Well, talking about it on the down low. One of my patients died, and I think he was killed. Just like the others."

"Thank you for coming. Please, have a seat and tell us about it." Rick gestures at the chair beside his desk.

Officer Fuentes nods once, and walks back to the front room.

Maya removes her coat, wads it in her lap, and sits. "Thanks. The man's name was Roger Matheson, one of my assigned patients. He was eighty, and suffering from inoperable liver cancer. I went in to check on him about 6:30 in the morning —this was last October—and found him unresponsive. Called in a code, but we weren't able to revive him. Officially, they declared his death cardiac arrest, but I think someone killed him with an epinephrine overdose. I found a bottle tossed in the trash at the nurse's station, stuffed inside a dirty lunch baggie."

"I'm guessing medical bottles aren't supposed to be tossed in the wastebasket there?"

She shakes her head at me. "Nope. Especially not covered in peanut butter. I reported it, but there's no way anyone could get fingerprints off it. Pretty sure whoever dropped it there did it in a rush, and smeared PB all over the bottle on purpose."

"Something must have spooked the guy," says Rick.

"Look, umm..." Maya bites her lip. "I don't have any proof, but you guys might want to look into a nurse named Lucas Porter. He comes off as really nice, but there's something about him that doesn't feel right. Like he's just some dude playing a character on TV. He acts sweet, but there's always that second or two when he first looks at you that just makes your skin crawl."

"This Porter... is he tall, bald, kinda biker-looking?" I ask.

"Well, everyone's tall to me." Maya grins. "But yeah. He's bald. I guess he looks like a biker, but those guys usually have beards and tats, right?"

"Horseshoe bald or Kojak bald?" asks Rick.

"Umm, what?" Maya blinks.

Rick chuckles. "Does he have a ring of hair around the back of his head or are we talking shiny skin job."

"Oh. Shiny." She nods. "No hair at all. When that other patient died, the one from the car accident, I had to speak up. Like I said, Mr. Matheson died in October. I'd only been an RN for nine months at the time, so the administration didn't take me too seriously when I said someone killed him. Eighty-year-old guy with terminal liver cancer having a heart attack didn't set off too many alarms in people's heads. I went to the administration again when that car accident patient died two weeks ago.

They're sorta-listening now, but they're not moving fast enough. This guy is going to kill again. I talked to Tina, my supervisor, about my concerns and she kinda dismissed me. Lucas is so nice and friendly, they don't think he could do anything like that. So... I remembered seeing you at the hospital and I decided to come here to talk to you."

Oh shit. I stare into space, thinking about what Jenna Harvey said. The nurse who she opened up to about being abused at home had been super nice. Shane hadn't been terminal, but he *had* represented a continuing threat to that woman and her children. Dr. Rahman was right. Shane Harvey's murder isn't actually an outlier to the MO. The killer *does* have a mercy complex. He hadn't been performing a mercy for Shane, but for Jenna and the children.

"Thank you so much for this information." I smile. "Would you be willing to testify if and when this hits a courtroom?"

"Absolutely. Oh..." Maya pulls out her phone. "I took pictures of the epi bottle. Want those?"

"Yeah. That might come in handy." Rick gives her our public email.

She fiddles with her phone for a minute or so. "Okay. Sent 'em. I don't know what the administration did with the bottle, but I didn't trust them so I took the pictures."

"Is there anything else you observed or know that might help us?" asks Rick.

Maya ponders for a moment, then shakes her head. "Nothing more than rumors."

"Has this Porter guy ever been caught in the room of a patient he's not been assigned to?" I lean over to my computer and open the email client. Several photos show a Ziploc baggie that contains a tiny glass bottle slathered in peanut butter. She took shots from several angles, one of which clearly shows the drug label as epinephrine.

"Not that I know of." She shakes her head. "Sorry."

"How long has he worked at Oaktree?" Rick turns to the next page in his notepad.

"A lot longer than me. Years, but I don't know exactly."

I nod.

We talk to her for a little while more, collecting her contact info and making sure she can't think of anything else that could prove helpful—not that what she gave us already wasn't awesome. After walking her out to the lobby, I race back to my desk and pull up everything I can find on Lucas Porter.

According to his driver's license, he's thirty-eight. Hair's listed as black, though he's completely shaved. He doesn't have a criminal record, but there is a note indicating a sealed juvenile record. Few traffic tickets, including one DUI which ended up being overturned. The patrol officer cited him for driving while intoxicated despite the breath test coming back negligible. In court, Porter argued that he hadn't been drinking, but rather exhausted from working long hours at the hospital. Since the breathalyzer test showed almost no alcohol in his system, the judge threw the DUI out.

Our other suspect, Gerald, also had a habit of showing up at work while groggy.

"Crap. No wonder they're part timers…"

Rick looks over at me.

"Gerald and William work part time because one guy can't be in three places simultaneously. He's chronically tired because he's working three jobs."

"Hang on." Rick points at my victim board. "Gerald Peters is like almost sixty, and William Johnston doesn't look anything like this guy. Where did you even get the notion they're the same person?"

"Caius blurted something, and it just clicked in my head, making total sense."

He stares at me.

"Yeah, I know how it sounds. But it feels right." My hair flops down over my face.

Rick chuckles. "You have to do that on purpose."

"Do what?"

"The hair thing. It makes you look, I dunno, whimsical. Whenever you really want me to believe you, your hair drapes over your eyes."

I pull it back off my face. "She has a mind of her own."

"Right." He leans back in his chair. "You know, if anyone else told me they got a hunch based on a random statement from someone completely unrelated to the case, I'd have laughed. With you,

I'm not so sure."

"You danced naked around a bonfire and talked to the Devil or something, Wims?" asks Linda Gonzalez in a surprisingly jovial tone for her.

"No, but I did happen to be nude at the time." I wink. "In bed with the fiancée."

She makes a gagging motion with her finger.

"I'm with Gonzales. Gross," says Rick. "And Mads, please tell me you're not expecting any sane judge to issue an arrest warrant based on 'my boyfriend said something at random while we had sex.'"

"Of course not. I do know the difference between what I think and what I can prove." I print out Lucas Porter's license portrait. "Let's take a quick ride."

***

Jenna Harvey answers the bell when I ring. She hides half behind the door for a moment before evidently remembering she doesn't need to be afraid of Shane anymore, and opens the door the rest of the way.

"Detectives? Umm, what made you drive all the way out here?"

"Hi." I smile and hand her a manila folder containing ten pictures of bald white guys. "We don't need to bother you for too long. I just wanted to know if you could tell me if the nurse you spoke to is in here."

She opens it and pages through, stopping on the fourth photo. "This is him."

Bingo. She picked Lucas Porter.

Rick nods.

"Would you be willing to say that in court?" I ask.

Jenna bites her lip. "I don't know. It feels like betraying him after what he did for us. Shane could've killed my kids, or me."

I nod. "I'm not going to try and claim his death was anything but good for you, but this man has killed at least six other people than your husband that we're aware of."

"Probably a lot more than that we don't know about yet," adds Rick.

"If we don't stop him, he's going to continue killing. You wouldn't need to say one way or the other if you think he killed Shane, just go on record identifying him."

Jenna looks down. "I guess. I'll think about it."

"All right. Thank you. That's all we needed to bother you with at the moment."

She nods and we say our goodbyes.

On the way back to the car, Rick looks over at me. "We could subpoena her."

"We could, but she's been through a lot already. I'd rather hold off unless we absolutely need to."

"Yeah. Guess we should get to work then."

I hop in the car. "Regular hours? What are those?"

He laughs.

Chapter Thirty
The Deadly Trinity

Quarrel is still so happy they found the clown killer, he ordered from a Mexican restaurant near the station, buying lunch for everyone.

I munch on a quesadilla while comparing the schedules and work times of William, Gerald, and Lucas courtesy of several phone calls to HR departments. It couldn't have been random for Caius to blurt about the Holy Trinity. He almost never talks about religion. That had to be a clue to me from whatever spirit or god prodded him with the information to pay attention.

More and more, I'm convinced that all three of these men are the same person… I just don't understand how that's possible… unless he's somehow using magic to make people see him differently. William and Gerald's driver's license photos both look a bit off... like uncanny valley. Ever look at like a robot trying to appear human but it's not quite there? Yeah, that's this picture. There's something about a human simulacrum when it's not perfect that feels creepy and unsettling. If a robot is *obviously* a robot, it doesn't unnerve people at all. The closer it gets to being human, the freakier it is. These men both kinda look not fully alive. It's possible they could be fake images. They gotta be. What are the odds I'm dealing with a paranormal serial killer?

Lucas's shift puts him at Oaktree Hospital from 6:00 a.m. to 3:00 p.m., Monday to Friday.

William works the night shift at Olympia Health Services Hospital part time from 11:00 p.m. to 5:00 a.m., Monday, Wednesday and Friday.

Gerald is also part time at Thurston County Ultimacare Pavilion from 6:00 p.m. to 2:00 a.m. on Saturday and Sunday.

Good grief. No wonder this guy is a zombie... if it's one person. Three days each week, he'd have an hour to go straight from the overnight shift at OHSH to his day shift at Oaktree. I call Rick over and point out the schedules. There wouldn't be much traffic on the road between five and six in the morning, but he'd have to employ some kind of disguise—or spell—to turn himself from thirty-year-old Lucas into sixty-year-old William.

"Damn. That would only leave the guy like four hours a day to sleep plus whatever naps he can slip in."

"They fired Gerald for being chronically late and groggy."

"Good point."

I arrange all three driver's license photos side by side to make it easier to compare them. William is slightly paunchy and somewhat paler than Lucas... plus he has short salt-and-pepper hair. Gerald is older with white hair, also pastier than Lucas and also a bit chubbier. Not to mention, Lucas is a lot younger. I stare at the pictures back and forth, my mind racing for an explanation. Lucas has the most normal-seeming picture. His face doesn't bug me as being unnatural.

"That nurse was right about Gerald. He does kinda look a bit off." Rick rubs his chin.

I focus on different parts of the face, comparing them one after the next.

They all have the same eyes. Same shade of brown, same shape.

"Rick, the eyes."

He leans close. "Oh, shit. You're right."

"I found a Gerald Peters who worked as an electrician in New Mexico years ago. He didn't look like this guy though. All the records checked out for someone having existed over there. I'm thinking some other person with the same name. Our Gerald Peters has got to be a fake identity. Gonna show this to Greer, see if we can get a search warrant for the residences."

"I'll check on his SSNs. If he faked those, that's another cherry on the sundae for the prosecutor."

"Okay." I hop up and rush across the room to the captain's office.

Greer looks at the photos for a few minutes before she winds up agreeing with me that they all have the same eyes. I go over Maya's information plus Jenna confirming Lucas had been the only one she told about Shane being violent with her and the kids.

"What's your thinking here?" asks Greer.

"Lucas is probably the real guy since he's the only one of the three working full time, at Oaktree. I'm thinking he follows a 'don't shit where you eat' policy—for the most part. That said, we still have two bodies I can connect to him at Oaktree, one a terminal eighty-year-old cancer patient, someone whose death wouldn't be at all suspicious. And Shane Harvey, who had to be an impulse decision after Lucas spoke with Jenna. He's been trying not to do his mercy killing act at his primary hospital to stay under the radar. Most of the deaths have occurred when he becomes William or Gerald. Maybe he's figuring he could simply drop the fake identity if the heat built up and still be in the clear as Lucas."

"You think this guy's gone totally off the farm? Personality disorder?"

I shake my head. "No. Too coordinated. Gerald's stealing drugs that William has killed with. If he had multiple personalities, they wouldn't necessarily know what the other one had been up to, and probably wouldn't even all be killers."

"Got something," he says. "Our Gerald Peters' social security number was issued to Gerald Peters, born in Albuquerque, New Mexico, in 1930. Died February eleventh, 1990. William Johnston's SSN was issued to William Johnson—no t—in New York, born November ninth 1982. The man is still alive. I have the strong suspicion that Porter forged a fake identity based on him. Anyone checking up on Johnston's past would see 'Johnson' in whatever documentation and probably assume it to be a typographical error.

"Bingo," says Greer. "Email me that. That's at least enough to get a peek inside this guy's house. Did you two ever check on the addresses for Gerald and William?"

"Not yet. Didn't want to spook the guy off." I glance at Rick. "Might as well take a quick ride."

He nods. "Let's go."

Chapter Thirty-One
Faces of Death

The address listed on Gerald's license doesn't exist. There's a 543 Pine Hollow Trail, and a 545 Pine Hollow Trail, but no 544.

Things like that happen with house numbers all the time, random skips or jumps. We check in at the nearest post office. The window clerk doesn't seem to know if 544 Pine Hollow Trail is real, but does tell us that Gerald has a mail forwarding to redirect anything sent there to a P.O. Box. Without a specific warrant to search that P.O. Box, we can't touch it, but it's probably irrelevant anyway. More than likely, the only mail he gets is junk or W2 forms.

William Johnston's apartment *does* exist, but a young-twenties black man with dreadlocks down to his butt—clearly *not* Johnston—answers the door.

We do the badge thing, introducing ourselves.

"Aww, shit." The guy fidgets. "What's this about?"

"Is this your apartment?" asks Rick.

"Yeah."

"Can you tell us your name, please?" I smile.

"Jared Edmonds."

I nod, writing that down. "How long have you lived here?"

"About a year. Kinda fuzzy on dates. Is something wrong?"

"Have you ever seen this man?" Rick holds up the photo of William Johnston.

"Uhh, yeah. Dude used to live here. Came by right after I moved in, said he was having a problem with the post office not forwarding his mail. Kept sending stuff here even though he moved out. Shit's *still* showin' up here. Dude swings by like once a month to pick it up. Gives me fifty bucks to hold onto it for him." He shrugs. "Free gas money, you know?"

"What sort of mail does he get?" I ask.

"Ehh, mostly junk mail. Sometimes he gets letters with like hospital marks on them. Hang on." Jared ducks inside to grab a cardboard box from a table near the door. "This is all the stuff that's waitin' for him."

We sift through mostly junk mail and two envelopes from Olympia Health Services Hospital. Nothing looks relevant to our investigation, so we chuck it back in the box and return it to Jared.

"Thanks for your time, Mr. Edmonds." I nod.

"What's up? This dude do something?"

"We're still trying to put all the pieces together," says Rick.

"When was the last time he showed up to collect his mail?"

"Umm." Jared ponders for a few seconds. "Like two weeks ago."

"Anything seem strange about him?" Rick pulls out his notepad.

"Not really. Just complaining about the post office still messing up his address change. Didn't seem to know when or if they'd ever fix it. Kinda weird though."

"What's weird?" I ask.

"Dude's tossin' me fifty bucks a month to hold his mail for him, instead of leanin' on the post office to fix it. I figured the guy might be up to something shady but, fifty bucks is fifty bucks and it ain't like I'm helping him move drugs or nothin'. Just junk mail and some other random shit."

"Yeah. That does sound weird." Rick smiles. "If you see him again, do us a favor and don't mention us."

"If?" asks Jared.

"There's some chance he might not be back. We'll probably return for that mail if that's the case."

"All right." He holds up a fist. "Peace out."

Rick and I both bump knuckles with him.

***

We head back to the station by way of a 'healthy' sandwich place.

Can't do heavy food *all* the time.

Alas, we end up inhaling our wraps in four bites because Greer handed us the warrant to search Lucas Porter's home. I fill her in on the fake addresses, then tell her about Johnston's mail. Some part of me—or maybe a little help from beyond—probably knew that those addresses were fake. No need for a warrant, since a resident at the premises gave us permission to go through the mail. Legal search, not that it turned up much.

That said, it strikes me as a bit weird we didn't look into the addresses earlier in the investigation. But finding bogus residences would have frustrated me beyond belief. Might have wound up surveilling Dreadlock guy's apartment and pouncing on William when he showed up to collect his mail. And that would've spooked the guy into dropping that identity. Or bailing, and living under yet another identity. Maybe even fleeing the state.

Leaving us with jack shit.

That's why The Goddess gave me a clue to treat this guy gently. Even more so now that I know Seattle detectives had already questioned 'Gerald' once. No doubt if Rick and I showed up to ask him, he'd be scared enough to vanish... and probably set up elsewhere. Thinking about how many deaths this guy could've gotten away with if not for that nurse Kaitlyn coming to talk to me makes me cringe. If

Porter slips through our hands, that could mean hundreds of victims.

So, yeah. I think things worked out here. Thank you to the Goddess and whatever other spirits contributed to my intuition.

Rick and I rush to Lucas's home address on Devon Loop, a suburban area in the northeast portion of Olympia. Two patrol units meet us there. No one answers the bell—or runs out the back door. So Rick uses the lock gun on the door and we go in, warrant metaphorically in hand. Our service weapons are actually in our hand.

A syrupy sweet smell hangs in the air reminding me of blueberry pancakes. The house is far too neat for a single guy's residence, looking mostly unoccupied. Given how much time this guy spends at various hospitals, that's unsurprising. I bet ninety percent of the time he's actually here, he's sleeping, showering, or eating... and, undoubtedly, planning his next murder.

The kitchen wastebasket contains mostly boxes from microwave meals, 'blueberry dream' breakfast at the top. Lucas's kitchen sink is a veritable monument of worship to coffee mugs. Seems the man's philosophy is to buy a new mug instead of washing the one he last used.

"Wims," says Rick, in front of the open fridge. "Bingo."

I hurry over and peer into a mostly-empty refrigerator. Behind one of two Chinese takeout containers is a small army of medicine bottles, the type with the rubber top that people stick needles through to load syringes.

"Epinephrine, Nembutal, digoxin…"

"Death just chilling out," says Rick. "Be right back."

I nod.

He runs to our car, returning with blue latex gloves and some evidence bags into which he transfers the meds. While he does that, I wander down a hallway deeper into the house. One of the patrol officers follows. Two empty rooms make searching quick. Upon reaching the master bedroom, I let out a tiny squeal of alarm at a ghastly sight.

The severed heads of Gerald and William stare at me from a long folding table set up against the wall on the right. It takes me a second or two to process that I'm not staring into the blank white eyes of mutilated corpses, but rather, full-face latex masks on Styrofoam heads. An elaborate cosmetics kit sits on the table between them under a big mirror. The room stinks of chemicals, which I assume are probably whatever adhesive he uses to keep the masks in place. My guess is rubber cement.

I take my department cell phone out and snap multiple photos of the makeup counter and both masks. While doing that, I locate two ID badges, one for Gerald Peters, one for William Johnston. There's also a ring with multiple small keys on it that might be for the other hospitals, but something tells me they open medicine lockers he shouldn't have access to. This is probably how he got into the pharmacy while Trevor ran to the bathroom.

"Hey Rick," I call. "Bring some baggies down here please."

"Sec!"

I keep taking pictures.

Eventually, Rick walks in, stuffing his phone back in the belt holder. "Just got off the line with Dr. Rahman. Two of those bottles match lot numbers stolen from Oaktree Hospital, and holy shit." He blinks at the masks. "That's only a *little* bit creepy."

"One guy. Three people." I gesture at the heads. "Lucas gets off work at five in the morning, races home, puts on the William face, and races to the other hospital all within one hour."

"Dude's crazy." Rick shakes his head.

"Yeah, that kinda goes without saying."

He grins. "Well, this is incriminating as all hell. I feel confident about picking him up. How about you?"

"Yep."

"Let's go offer him a ride downtown."

We ask the patrol officers to stay here and keep the site secure until we can come back and properly catalog everything related to the case.

That can wait until we get this guy off the street.

Chapter Thirty-Two
Time to Go

We arrive at Oaktree Hospital six minutes after two in the afternoon.

Lucas should be on shift at this hour. I don't expect he'll be armed or even particularly dangerous when confronted. Still, doesn't hurt to be prepared, so we've brought tasers just in case he puts up a fight. Our backup arrives a few minutes after us. Rick hands a printout of Lucas's ID photo to the four uniformed officers and sends them to each of the hospital's exits.

Staff, visitors, and some patients watch us, curious spectators wondering what the heck is about to go down, but no one approaches to ask questions. Once the uniforms head off to watch the doors, I approach the information desk in the lobby.

"Can I help you?" asks the woman there,

seeming a bit nervous.

I hold up my badge. "We're looking for a nurse named Lucas Porter. Can you tell us where he is in the hospital at the moment?"

"Umm. One sec." She picks up a phone and asks someone named Neal to get out here now.

Neal, a late-forties guy in a business suit, shows up a moment later. "What's going on?"

"The police are looking for one of the nurses." The young woman gestures at us.

"Where can we find Lucas Porter?" asks Rick.

"I'm not sure exactly. You'd want to check with the managing nurse on duty. That would be Betty Parker. You can find her on the second floor, B wing. Just go up that elevator over there, hang a left, and go straight to the big green desk."

"Thanks." I nod at him and head off toward the elevator.

Rick punches the button for the second floor. "You know, we could always have the hospital page him."

"Do they typically page nurses, or just doctors? Wouldn't that tip him off?"

"Maybe."

Ding.

The doors slide open.

I stride out into the hall and go left, adjusting my jacket to keep it out of the way of the taser I don't usually carry. An assortment of empty wheelchairs and carts litter the corridor, tucked up against the wall on both sides between doors to patient rooms. The desk Neal mentioned is about fifty yards down at an intersection with a crossing hallway.

Maya Britton, the nurse who showed up at the station, emerges from a patient room on the left, gives us a quick glance, and keeps going for two steps before recognition sets in. She stops and stares at us. "Hey. What's up? Are you looking for me?"

"No." I shake my head. "Do you know where Lucas is?"

Her eyes widen. "Oh damn…"

"Yeah. It's like that."

Rick chuckles.

Maya twists around to glance toward the nurse's station. "He should be down that way. His route is to the right from the desk. Need me to do anything?"

"Yeah," says Rick. "Just keep on doing whatever you should be doing."

She backs off to the side, leaning against the wall as if to give us extra room. "Okay."

I walk faster down the hallway and hook a right by the giant green desk. Another corridor stretches way off to a set of double doors. At least thirty rooms lie ahead, along with a smaller nurse station and a few closets.

Starting with the first room on the left, I peek in each doorway only long enough to check for Lucas. Right as I peek into the fifth room, Rick grabs my arm and tugs. I back out into the hall, but before I can ask him what's up, I spot a guy in teal scrubs going into another room six doors farther down the hall.

I run to the doorway, making entry with my hand on the taser.

A broad-shouldered man of average height, shiny bald, has his back to me, standing beside the bed of an elderly woman who doesn't appear conscious. He's doing something to the IV line coming off her arm. No freakin' way.

"Lucas Porter!" I call out. "Police. Back away from the bed and keep your hands where I can see them.

He freezes.

"Do it," says Rick in a loud, authoritative tone.

Lucas remains motionless.

I draw the taser, putting the laser sight dot on his back. "Now. Don't make me tase you."

"Nice and easy," says Rick. "Back away from the old lady and keep your hands in view."

"Is there a problem here?" asks a woman behind us.

Lucas spins around.

The sudden motion spooks me into pulling the trigger.

My taser barbs fly straight and true—right into the meal tray Lucas swings around to protect his chest. A half-consumed bottle of milk goes flying and splashes across the floor. No readable emotion on his face, Lucas rushes toward me, still holding the tray up like a shield. Rick squeezes off his taser, but one dart hits the tray, the other snags in Lucas's smock, evidently not hitting flesh. The snapping noise of useless electricity is the loudest sound in the universe for two seconds.

Lucas raises a syringe like a dagger, coming straight at me. I toss the spent taser aside and catch his wrist in both hands. His mass shoves me back into the doorjamb, which nails me between the shoulder blades. Oh, that's gonna bruise. It takes all my strength to hold the needle away from my neck, my shoes sliding on the polished floor. If not for the metal against my back, I'd end up on my ass. A knee to the balls might help, but I'm too worried about that needle to weaken my stance.

He's got the most eerie look in his eyes, a faint bit of a smile on his lips, as if he's merely observing nice flowers in a garden somewhere—or nobody's home inside. Rick also tosses his taser... and pulls his Glock. Lucas swings me to the left, putting me in the path of any shot Rick could take. My arms start to give out under his greater strength, the tip of the syringe inching closer to my throat.

Rick sticks his Glock past my head, pointing it at Lucas's eye from two inches away. "Drop the god damned needle!"

My hair flaps forward like an angry squid, covering Lucas's face, blinding him—and me—momentarily. He sputters, trying to shake his head back and forth. I lean to the side, swinging his arm down in a jiu-jitsu maneuver. My technique suffers from being too focused on keeping that syringe away from my skin, so he doesn't end up face down on the floor. However, psychotic or not, pain compliance works. A little pressure at the wrist and his hand involuntarily pops open, allowing the syringe to fall. Rick angles around, trying to get a hold of the guy.

Lucas grunts, twisting and grabbing at me. He shoves me into Rick and takes off running down the hallway. I crash into my partner, my shoulder nailing him in the abdomen. It's like hitting a wall of sandbags, though he does emit an *oof.*

"Dammit," mutters Rick, deciding not to shoot an unarmed guy in the back.

A skinny Indian woman in a doctor's coat—likely the one who distracted us by asking if we had a problem—starts shouting at someone down the corridor to page security.

I recover my balance and leap away from Rick, chasing Lucas. I'm expecting him to go for the double doors and a stairwell out, but he surprises me by darting left into a room near the end of the hall and slamming the door.

Naturally, by the time I get to it, he's locked it. 'Storage B-4' is stenciled on the plain wood in black letters.

I point at the doctor shouting about security. "Does this closet have a window?"

She shakes her head.

Rick slides to a halt beside me and tries the knob—as if I didn't just do that. "Come on, man. Don't make this any harder than it has to be."

An agonized scream comes from the closet.

"Open this!" I turn toward the doctor. "You have keys for this closet?"

She shakes her head and beckons over one of the nurses, who comes running, pulling a massive tangle of keys out of her smock pocket. I've never seen anyone pick out a specific key so fast from a mess like that. The woman's good under pressure, no doubt.

The *thump* of a body hitting the floor comes from behind the door, along with more groaning and gasping.

"He's injected himself," I yell. I look at the nurse. "Hurry! Open this damn door."

The nurse stabs the key into the lock and gives it a twist.

I barge past her into a closet full of linens and cleaning supplies. Lucas is flat on his back in the middle of the windowless space, twitching, a syringe hanging from his left arm. His face has gone red and he's gulping for air like a fish out of water. I dart in and search his pockets, finding a bottle of Nembutal, which I toss to the nurse.

She runs to a box on the wall, hits an alarm, and dashes over to an empty gurney. "Help me get him up."

Rick and I haul Lucas off the floor, moving him to the gurney. The doctor and several more nurses run over. We jog along, hanging back a little from the medical team rushing him down the hall to a room where they intubate him and hook him up to a respirator. It doesn't look like he's going anywhere

269

soon, so we leave them to it before anyone chases us out, and wait in the hall.

"Well, that could've gone better," mutters Rick.

"Could've gone worse, too."

"True. Yeah. Definitely true."

Chapter Thirty-Three
Inescapable Suffering

Two days later, Rick and I walk down the hall to Lucas Porter's hospital room.

The patrol officer on guard duty stands, grinning at me when I hand him a large coffee. Figured there'd be a cop here, so we got an extra coffee on our way over. We chitchat with him for a little while, bringing him up to speed on the plan to transfer Lucas to county later that day once the doctor signs off on his medical release.

Nembutal kills by paralyzing the diaphragm, causing the victim to suffocate. They kept him alive by mechanical respiration until the drug ran its course. The past day or so has been mostly observation for any complications.

We step into the room to find Lucas watching television. Other than his being handcuffed to the bed frame, he looks no different from any other patient, even in good spirits. Though he does have that same creepy smile.

Rick reads him his Miranda rights before we pull out our notepads.

I also set up a digital recorder. "You don't need to tell us anything, but we'd appreciate it. Also, I hereby inform you that this conversation is being recorded into evidence. That said... why?"

He shrugs one shoulder. "I had to. It's my calling."

"Your calling?" asks Rick.

"When I was seventeen, I decided that my existence was a mistake, so I tried to end my life. My suicide attempt would have succeeded if not for the intervention of a higher power. I jumped off a seventy-foot bridge. Only broke a few bones. Most people who jumped from that place died on impact. Obviously, He did not want me to die yet, keeping me on this earth to do what people should do but cannot. Alleviate suffering."

"So you believe that God commanded you to kill?" asks Rick.

"Except for that one man, I did not kill. There is no reason to subject people to inescapable suffering when their deaths are inevitable. It twists the mind and warps the spirit. They deserved dignity in the afterlife, so I merely expedited the natural process already in place."

"Except for that one man?" Rick tilts his head. "Which man? Bear in mind you are being recorded."

"Shane Harvey. He tortured his wife and children. That poor little boy was so frightened. It was only a matter of time before the man murdered one or all of them. While it is my primary calling to ease the suffering of those God calls to his domain, I could not in good conscience allow an agent of Satan to remain on this Earth and harm the innocent."

"What did you do about this 'agent of Satan'?" I ask.

"The same thing I did to myself two days ago. Pancuronium bromide, or Nembutal. I chose that to end his life because it is excruciatingly painful. For all the pain he inflicted upon those innocent people."

I raise both eyebrows. "Do you believe you deserved such a painful end?"

"No thought of that kind went into the matter. The Nembutal is the only thing I had on me at the time."

"You are aware that you have just confessed to the murder of Shane Harvey?" I ask.

"I am. It doesn't matter." Lucas smiles at us like we're discussing a painting he made, not a murder. "It is apparently God's will that my work comes to an end at this time. I will tell you about the others as well."

We sit and listen as he iterates through names of various patients he administered lethal injections to, including eleven more we hadn't heard of yet, like

Edna Majors: a sixty-eight-year-old stroke patient who he killed (as William) via digoxin. Her death was ruled cardiac arrest. The guy speaks with an eerie, clinical detachment as though he's merely talking about helping old people cross the street, not killing human beings.

"The doctors did not expect her to ever wake. She had suffered such a severe ischemic attack, little remained of her higher brain functions," says Lucas. "It would have been crueler to allow her to suffer in mute silence for however many years she lingered."

"Wow." Rick looks at his pad, and list of names.

"Detectives." Lucas smiles that weird little smile again. "I must tell you. I am still eager to leave this world behind. Only my work helping others has kept me going. Without it, I have no reason to remain alive. If I am incarcerated, unable to assist those in need, I will go to Him."

"Excuse me," says Rick. "But if you were supposed to check out, wouldn't God have kept that door locked long enough for you to depart? I don't think he wants you to die just yet."

Lucas swallows, his gaze drifting off us into space. "So what happens now?" he asks a moment or two later, his tone distant and lifeless.

"Well, you're looking at murder charges for at least eight counts," I say.

"That can't be right. There are at least thirty. I have the names at home on my computer. I print memorial cards for them."

"All right." Rick closes his notepad. "Once the doctors release you, we'll be taking you to processing. You'll have an attorney appointed to represent you unless you wish to hire one privately."

"I understand," says Lucas.

"Oh, one more question, Mr. Porter," I say. "If you are doing God's work, why the disguises and alternate identities?"

"To stay one step ahead of Satan," says Lucas, without hesitation.

I blink. "You consider us Satan?"

"I don't hold it against you. Most people don't even realize the dark one pulls their strings. Police do perform a valuable service, but you cannot see that my work is of a divine mandate. Therefore, I needed to do what I could to stay one step ahead of the Devil when he manipulates the police into interfering with me."

"You know," says Rick, "people used to believe people with red hair were sent by Satan."

I shake my head.

"Get some sleep, Lucas," I say, picking up the digital recorder. "You won't be working sixteen hours a day anymore."

He settles into the pillow. "See you soon, detectives."

As we walk out into the hall, I mouth 'wow.'

Rick chuckles. "Think the lawyer will try to plead insanity?"

"He will if he thinks it'll give Lucas a chance to go free sooner."

"Thirty victims? Asylum or prison, that guy's done." Rick shakes his head. "C'mon, let's go check that computer."

"Wait. I'm having another bit of precognition." I touch my fingers to my temples. "We're going to be working late tonight."

Laughing, Rick pokes the button for the elevator. "Yeah. No shit."

Chapter Thirty-Four
External Interference

I end up driving while Rick gets on the phone with Greer to arrange transport for Porter. She warns us that a crowd of roughly a hundred demonstrators somehow got wind of the 'death angel nurse' as the media's started calling him, and doesn't want us using the front door. With any luck, we'll take him out a service entrance in a bullet-proof vest.

"Will do," says Rick, about to hang up. "What's that?"

Greer's voice murmurs from the phone for a moment.

"Aww, shit, really?" asks Rick. "Copy that, Captain." He hangs up and punches an address into the GPS. "Slight detour."

"What happened?" I ask.

"Jumper. Shouldn't take too long. Just need us to check it out and sign off on it being a suicide."

I groan. "Another jumper?"

"Well, we *are* close to Seattle."

"What's that supposed to mean?"

"Not everyone likes the rain, Mads."

I roll my eyes. "Okay, let's go."

***

Ten minutes later, I pull over and park by a cluster of patrol cars. Uniformed officers have the area at the base of a high-rise office tower cordoned off. Much like roughly two weeks ago, a body lays on the sidewalk under a tarp. Streaks of blood smear the sidewalk past where the blue plastic covers.

We get out of the car and walk over to the sergeant.

"What'cha got?" asks Rick.

"Weird one." The guy shakes his head. "A couple of witnesses from the upper floor offices say they heard the guy screaming 'get off me' before he fell, then screamed 'no' for half the way down."

"Half?" asks Rick.

The cop shrugs. "Probably lost consciousness at that point."

I glance toward the body… and a cold, serpentine touch glides down my back. Something dark catches my eye, sinking into the space between this building and the next.

"Okay, we'll check it out," says Rick, then starts

walking to the building, pausing when I don't follow him.

I keep watching the alley, but whatever it was doesn't reappear. A similar feeling hits me like what happened at the other site. Gah, that feels so long ago. These two men are connected, and I don't think they jumped on their own.

"Wims?"

Still watching the alley, I edge over to stand beside him and mutter, "He was pushed..."

"Great. So much for being quick."

"... by something supernatural."

Rick hangs his head. "Shit."

"Yeah. Shit is right." I take a step toward the body. "Let me see if the guy has anything to say."

"Wims, sometimes, you can really creep a guy out."

I brace myself and peel back the sheet. Oof. Poor bastard. Gingerly, I reach out and put a finger on his cheek. He hasn't been dead long enough for the body to become completely cold. A trace of dark energy lingers within the remains, but not enough for me to get any insight or visions from.

Great. Why do I have a feeling this is going to turn into the supernatural version of the clown case?

No, this is going to be worse. Officially, they're all going down as suicides.

That means I'm not going to be able to work this investigation on the books. Even suggesting what's most likely the truth here would likely cause a mandatory meeting with the department psychiatrist and I'd *still* not be allowed to log these two deaths as homicides. Even Rick's probably going to think I'm going too far out on a limb if I start talking about 'dark spirits' forcing people to kill themselves. But I can't simply allow this to continue. I've got to do something even if I'm on my own.

This is going to suck.

"Anything?" asks Rick.

Annoyed, I stand, shaking my head. "Only suspicions I can't put in any report."

"So, another suicide."

I glance up at the roof. "It certainly appears that way."

"Okay, pal. What can you tell me?"

The End

Maddy Wimsey returns in:
The Queens's Gambit
by J.R. Rain and
Matthew S. Cox
Coming Soon!

About J.R. Rain:

J.R. Rain is the international bestselling author of over seventy novels, including his popular Samantha Moon and Jim Knighthorse series. His books are published in five languages in twelve countries, and he has sold more than 3 million copies worldwide.

Please find him at: www.jrrain.com.

~~~

About Matthew S. Cox:

Originally from South Amboy NJ, **Matthew S. Cox** has been creating science fiction and fantasy worlds for most of his reasoning life. Since 1996, he has developed the "Divergent Fates" world, in which Division Zero, Virtual Immortality, The Awakened Series, The Harmony Paradox, and the Daughter of Mars series take place.

Matthew is an avid gamer, a recovered WoW addict, Gamemaster for two custom systems, and a fan of anime, British humour, and intellectual science fiction that questions the nature of reality, life, and what happens after it.

He is also fond of cats.

Please find him at: www.matthewcoxbooks.com

Made in the USA
Middletown, DE
29 December 2022